Death at Devil's Bridge

Death at
Devil's Bridge

CYNTHIA DEFELICE

FARRAR, STRAUS AND GIROUX

NEW YORK

Copyright © 2000 by Cynthia DeFelice
All rights reserved
Distributed in Canada by Douglas & McIntyre Ltd.
Printed in the United States of America
Designed by Filomena Tuosto
First edition, 2000
10 9 8 7 6 5 4 3 2 1

Library of Congress Cataloging-in-Publication Data
DeFelice, Cynthia C.
    Death at Devil's Bridge / Cynthia DeFelice — 1st ed.
        p.   cm.
    Summary: Despite a great summer job as first mate on a fishing boat
out of Martha's Vineyard, thirteen-year-old Ben gets caught up with
illegal drugs and possible murder.
    ISBN 0-374-31723-2
    [1. Drugs—Fiction.   2. Fishing—Fiction.   3. Martha's Vineyard
(Mass.)—Fiction.]   I. Title.

PZ7.D3597 Dc 2000
[Fic]—dc21   99-056097

FOR HELEN MANNING,
QUEEN OF THE CLIFFS

Death at Devil's Bridge

One

THE SUMMER WAS crazy right from the beginning, even before I discovered the sunken car in West Basin harbor. The *Gazette* was reporting "record numbers" of tourists pouring from the ferry boats onto Martha's Vineyard, the island where I lived. Mom was working all weekend at Town Hall, selling them beach passes. Barry Lester, the guy who'd been kind of her boyfriend since Pop died, was busy renting them cars and mopeds and Jeeps. And I had my first real job.

I was working for Pop's old friend Chick Flanders, who owned a bait and tackle store down-island in Edgartown. Chick used to be a commercial fisherman, like Pop. When the bad years hit the commercial fishery, Chick quit fishing and bought the bait shop. But it turned out he couldn't stand being indoors behind the cash register all day.

"Ben," he said, "it drives me crazy to talk about fishing instead of doing it. If your father was alive, he'd have told me straight out I was being a bonehead to buy the store. 'Chick,' he'd have said, 'you're a fisherman, not a shop-keeper.' " Chick shook his head and grinned.

I nodded, imagining Pop saying it. There were lots of things I liked about being with Chick, and one was that he wasn't afraid to talk about Pop. It was weird the way some people avoided the subject and were scared to even mention fathers or dying. Which was really stupid. They didn't want to remind me that Pop was dead, as if I never thought about it unless somebody slipped and brought it up. But Chick talked about Pop whenever he felt like it, and I liked hearing the old stories about them growing up and fishing together.

Anyway, Chick had finally admitted he was a bonehead, hired somebody to watch the shop, and began taking out charters on his boat *Something Fishy*. He had all four days of the upcoming Fourth of July weekend booked, and asked me if I wanted to be his first mate. I jumped at the chance.

Fishing with Chick wasn't the same as being with Pop, not exactly. But there was something familiar about the way Chick handled the boat, the way he moved and thought. Chick counted on me to know what I was doing, for the most part, and I liked the way he taught me new stuff without making a big deal out of it.

Not only that, but I was going to get paid thirty dollars a day, which I thought was pretty good for a thirteen-year-old kid. By Monday night, I'd have made a hundred and twenty dollars, more if I got tips. When I told that to my best friend, Jeff Manning, his eyes just about bugged out of his head.

One hundred twenty dollars was a lot of money, but we needed a lot more if we were ever going to be able to buy the fourteen-foot aluminum skiff with the twenty-five horsepower motor we wanted. Jeff and I planned to work really hard over the summer to get closer to having that boat.

Being first mate meant that I got the rods and bait ready in the morning, cleaned the fish we caught, washed up the boat at the end of the day, and kept the cooler stocked with ice and drinks. Piece of cake.

But Chick explained that working on a charter boat isn't only about fishing. "You get all kinds of people," he said. "They're paying for a good time, and you've got to stay on your feet and figure out how to keep them happy. Some of them know what they're doing with a rod in their hands, but a lot of them don't. You might have to help people bait their hooks, show them how to cast, maybe even hook a fish and reel it in for them."

"No way!" I said. I couldn't remember a time when I hadn't known how to catch fish.

"You wait and see," Chick said, laughing. Then his face grew serious and he added, "It's one thing when people don't know how to fish. But every once in a while you get a guy who's a real pain in the tail. When that happens, you just have to bite your tongue and be polite."

I grinned at him. "You mean I have to suck up to people even if they're real jerks?"

Chick smiled and shook his head. "I didn't say that. Just don't let 'em get to you. Keep your cool, and get through the day. Blow off steam to me later. Got it?"

"Got it," I said.

On my first day out with Chick, I learned he sure was right about one thing: knowing how to handle fish was only part of the job. The easy part. Knowing how to handle people was a lot trickier.

It was Friday of the Fourth of July weekend, and our clients were Bill and Ann Brewster and their four kids. They seemed nice enough, but I wasn't sure the kids were going to make it through a whole day in the boat. Two of them were fighting over who got to sit in the chair next to what they called the "steering wheel," one was complaining that he didn't *want* to go fishing, he wanted to go to the beach, and the littlest one, a girl, kept saying, "My tummy feels funny, Mommy. Mommy, it *hurts.*"

We were leaving the dock at West Basin harbor. There's a sandbar between the dock and the channel where a couple of boats run aground every year. I was standing on the bow, looking into the water to make sure we were going to clear the bar, and, suddenly, *there it was*. Through the ripples on the surface, I could see, sitting on the sandy bottom almost right under the boat, a bright red *car*.

"Cut the engine!" I shouted.

As I hollered to Chick, I drew my finger across my throat in a gesture that he was sure to understand even if he couldn't hear me above the sound of the motor. By then I had decided the tide was high enough that we were in no danger of hitting the sandbar, but I wasn't sure we could clear the roof of a car, and I didn't want Chick to ram it with the hull or the propeller.

In the sudden silence, Chick looked at me with a puzzled frown. "What?" he asked.

"There's a *car* down there," I said. It sounded really dumb when I said it. I mean, you might expect to see a sunken boat in the harbor, but a car? Still, there it was beneath the shimmering surface, big and red and as real as the bow line in my hand.

All at once the thought flashed into my mind: *What if*

there's somebody in there? Without really thinking about it, I kicked off my boots and jumped into the water. The boat had drifted, so I had to swim for about twenty yards to get back to the car. I dived down, then opened my eyes to look in the window. I was filled with sudden terror at the idea of someone looking back at me, someone dead, with swollen, bulging eyes. But there was no one.

I shot to the surface and swam over to the stern, where Chick gave me a hand climbing into the boat. "Nobody in it," I said, gasping.

"Looks like somebody drove right off the boat ramp," said Chick.

I nodded. West Basin was kind of a weird place, I figured. Lobsterville Road just ended there, and turned into an unpaved ramp where you could launch a boat off a trailer into the harbor. Everybody who lived there was used to it, but it surprised a lot of tourists who thought the road ought to *go* somewhere, such as across the channel to the village of Menemsha, instead of dead-ending in the water.

"What are you going to do, Captain?" asked Mr. Brewster.

"We've got to go over to Squid Row to get gas, anyway," Chick said, pointing to the neighboring Menemsha harbor.

Menemsha was much larger than West Basin. That was

where the big commercial fishing ships docked, along with all kinds of other fishing and pleasure boats. There was a gas dock and a store where you could buy bait, tackle, drinks, and snacks.

"We'll report the car to the harbormaster," Chick went on. "Then we'll go fishing."

And that was what we did. It was a pretty wild day's fishing, too. The kids went nuts when their dad brought in a big beauty of a striper. It was the first real, live fish they'd ever seen, I guessed, and they all wanted to catch one, too. They began casting their baited hooks in all directions, getting them stuck on the bottom, wedged under rocks, and caught in gobs of seaweed. The *Something Fishy* was twenty-four feet long, but it began to feel awfully small, especially when the youngest boy whipped his rod out behind him to cast and hooked me right under the chin. Luckily, it didn't go in past the barb, but it still hurt a lot.

"Hey!" I cried. "You're supposed to catch the fish, not the people!"

He thought that was hilarious, and pretended to try to hook me again. He was only fooling around, but it got a little hairy. Finally, his father made him sit in the "time-out" chair for five minutes. I'd always thought that was really dumb when Mom made me do it, but right then the time-out chair struck me as an excellent idea.

What with ducking to avoid flying hooks and chunks of slimy mackerel, baiting and untangling lines, netting fish, and keeping the boat in the correct position, Chick and I had our hands full.

I didn't have time to think about the sunken car until we headed into Menemsha harbor at four o'clock that afternoon.

Two

WE CAME IN with a pretty decent catch: four keeper bass and three big blues. A small crowd gathered as we unloaded the fish, and stayed to watch me clean them. Everybody likes to go out with a successful captain, and Chick signed up a couple more charters for the next week from among the onlookers. When the Brewsters left, looking tired and sunburned and happy, each kid was holding a dripping bag of fresh fish fillets as a souvenir of the trip.

I began cutting bait for the next day. Chick was fiddling with the bilge pump, which had quit during the afternoon, when Pete Vanderhoop, the Menemsha harbormaster, walked over.

"You missed all the excitement," he said dryly. "Jim

hauled the thing out with one of his tow trucks. It was a brand-new, mid-engine Porsche. Can you beat that?"

I wasn't sure what "mid-engine" meant, but I did know that a Porsche was a pretty hot sports car.

Chick whistled. "Big bucks down the drain."

"Yes, and the strange thing is, there's no sign of the owner."

"He's probably too embarrassed to show his face," I said.

"I would be, too, if I drove into the drink," Chick commented. "It wasn't an island car, was it?"

Pete shook his head. "It had Connecticut license plates."

"Well," said Chick, "by now the police have probably run the plate numbers and found out who it's registered to."

"Probably," Pete agreed. "The other interesting thing is that the cops are pretty sure there wasn't anybody driving when it went in the water."

"How do they know?" I asked.

"Well, the side windows were open a little, and so was the sunroof—just enough to sink it pretty fast, but not enough for someone to climb out. And both doors were closed."

I waited, not sure what Pete was getting at.

"Ed was saying that it would be nearly impossible to

open a car door against the weight of all that water." Ed Widdiss was the police chief for the town of Aquinnah, which included West Basin. "And even if somebody did get the door open, you think he'd take the time to close it behind him?"

I thought about that. It was a good question. "But if nobody was driving, how did it get in the water?" I asked.

"Ed figures it might have rolled in by accident. Or somebody could have pushed it in for a prank."

"Pretty expensive prank," Chick observed.

"Well, this time of year, with all these people around, I guess anything can happen," Pete said.

"Not like the good old days when tourists didn't get up-island much," said Chick. "Now they rent cars and those blasted mopeds and—" His face reddened and he broke off, probably remembering that Mom's boyfriend, Barry, owned the biggest car-and-moped rental agency on the island.

But I knew what Pete meant. The thing about living in Martha's Vineyard was that it was really like living in two different places. For most of the year, it was pretty quiet, and you knew just about everybody you ran into. Then— *bam!* Summer came, and the island was crawling with strangers. Suddenly there were traffic jams and lines at the grocery store and crowds on the beaches. There were so many more tourists than islanders that sometimes it felt as if they were taking over, as if the island was more their place than ours. And every summer got worse than the one before.

Chick and Pete continued to shoot the breeze while I hosed down the boat with fresh water and Chick finished fixing the pump. Then Chick and I motored back across the channel and tied up for the night at the West Basin dock.

"Nice job today, Ben," Chick said, handing me my thirty dollars. "Did I see Mr. Brewster give you a tip?"

"Yep," I said proudly, patting my pocket. "Ten bucks."

"Good," said Chick, smiling. "You earned it."

"That's for sure!" Warily I asked, "Are there going to be little kids on board again tomorrow?"

Chick laughed. "No. Two big kids, as a matter of fact."

"Whew!" I said. "I just wondered if I needed to bring safety goggles and a helmet!" I headed for my bike, calling back, "See you tomorrow."

Pedaling up Lobsterville Road toward home, I could tell that summer was really here: the West Basin parking lot was full of cars I didn't recognize. But coming toward me was a junker I'd have known anywhere. It was an old blue Pontiac LeMans—at least it had started out blue. Now its dented side panels were covered with body filler and primer paint in all kinds of colors. Actually, I thought, you'd have to say that the car was mainly silver, from the dull gleam of duct tape, which was plastered everywhere and which, I figured, was what mostly held the car together.

Across the front and rear bumpers, the word "Tomahawk" was spelled out in duct tape letters. That was to remind everyone that the owner, Donny Madison, like Jeff, was a member of the Wampanoag Indian tribe and proud of it. "Nobody messes with the Tomahawk," Donny liked to say.

Donny slowed and stopped beside me, his brown, muscled arm hanging out the Tomahawk's window, keeping time to the music blaring from the radio. "Ben, my man!" he said. "How goes it?"

"Hey, Donny," I said. Looking in the car, I expected to see Jen Navarro, Donny's girlfriend, snuggled close beside him. To my surprise, it was my best friend, Jeff, sitting in the passenger seat, his arm hanging out the other window, looking quite pleased with himself.

"Hi, Ben," he called over the pounding of the speakers.

I looked at him and lifted an eyebrow. I figured Jeff knew me well enough to read my mind: *Think you're pretty hot stuff driving around with Donny, don't you, Manning? How'd you get so lucky, anyway?*

Donny said to me, "Word is, you've got yourself a job." His face wore its usual expression: eyes half-shut and lazy looking, mouth grinning at me as if we shared some kind of secret, something funny or wild only the two of us knew. Which made me feel great, because Donny was cool.

For one thing, he knew everything about cars. For another thing, when Donny was around, things happened. If there was something exciting or a little bit edgy going on, Donny was usually right in the middle of the action. That made him popular with the kids, but got him into a lot of trouble at school, and the minute he turned sixteen, he dropped out.

The town of Aquinnah was so small, everybody knew everything about everybody else, and since my mom worked at Town Hall, she heard all the news eventually, usually before anyone else. When she heard about Donny quitting school, she gave me a big lecture about how important education is, and said Donny was headed for nothing but trouble.

I was sure she'd never let me go driving around in the Tomahawk with Donny, even if he'd asked me to, which he hadn't. I'd have bet the forty dollars in my pocket that Jeff's mother didn't know where *he* was at that moment, but that didn't stop me from wishing I was in his place.

"Yeah," I said to Donny. "I do have a job. I'm mating for Chick. Just for four days, more if he stays busy."

Donny batted his eyelashes and raised his voice to a

high falsetto. "Oooh, Mister First Mate, could you please put this bait on my hook for me? It's so *icky.*"

I laughed and said, "Talk about icky, this morning a little girl threw up all over the place."

"Gross," said Jeff.

"She actually turned green," I added.

"Let me guess," said Donny, smiling widely now. "It was the mate's job to clean it up."

"You got that right," I said, making a face.

"Poor kid," Donny said. Then he added, "I mean her, Daggett, not you. Cleaning up barf is good for you. Builds character."

"Great," I said. "I'll remember that. Hey, did you hear about that mid-engine Porsche in West Basin?" I threw in "mid-engine" to impress Donny, and hoped Jeff wouldn't blow it and ask me what it meant.

Donny grinned wickedly. "Some little rich boy's daddy is going to be plenty tee'd off."

"Oh, wow," I said. "You mean you know whose car it is?"

Donny smiled again and said, "No. But it stands to reason it's some fat cat tourist's, right? Who else drives a car like that? Not one of us local boys, eh?" He reached down and patted the door of the Tomahawk. "Our cars have *class.*"

Jeff reached a hand out and patted the Tomahawk's other door, almost as if he owned it. "Definitely!" he said.

I stared at Jeff, amazed at how cool he was acting. I felt like a little weenie, standing in the road, straddling my bike, while he sat shotgun in the Tomahawk as if he belonged there. "You know," I blurted, "I'm the one who saw it first."

"No way!" exclaimed Jeff. "You found the car?"

"Really?" Donny's eyebrows lifted with interest. "When?"

Pleased at having their full attention, I tried to sound casual. "First thing this morning. Chick and I were headed out and all of a sudden I saw this car in the water. I couldn't believe it!"

"Yeah, well, believe it, Daggett," said Donny. He reached out his hand to give me a high five. "And the rich kids who come here thinking they're better than us— they'd best believe it, too. Right, Manning?" he added, turning to Jeff and high-fiving him, too.

"You got it!" said Jeff.

Just then there was a loud beep, and I looked up to see a car coming our way, heading in the same direction as Donny. I scrambled to get out of the road so the car could go by. I caught a glimpse of the driver, a guy with a long gray ponytail. He scowled at me impatiently, then gave Donny a slow nod as he passed.

Donny gunned the engine. "Catch ya later, Daggett."

"Later, Ben," called Jeff as they pulled away.

"Right," I said, watching them disappear around a curve in the road. "Later."

Geez, I thought, *I work for one day and Jeff goes and finds a new best friend.*

Three

"HI, BEN," MOM CALLED from the kitchen. "How was your first day of work?"

"Okay," I answered, opening the refrigerator door, then pouring a glass of milk. "I guess you heard about the car."

"Such a waste," Mom said, shaking her head. "I almost fainted when Chief Widdiss told me how much a car like that costs. He says it'll never run again after being in the saltwater all night."

"Did he tell you I was the first one to see it?" I asked, grabbing two cookies from the jar on the counter.

"No more of those," Mom warned. "You'll spoil your dinner. I'm making tacos."

"Cool," I said. "Is Barry coming over?"

"Not for dinner," Mom answered. "He's too busy with all the holiday-weekend rentals. He might stop over later."

There was a time when I'd have been really happy to hear Barry wasn't coming for dinner. I even used to have a secret nickname for him: Barry the Bozo. But I didn't call him that anymore. I'd changed my mind about Barry during last year's fishing derby, when he was the one who proved that Freddy Cobb had cheated by adding mercury to his big striper to make it weigh more. Barry had saved the whole tournament, and Pop's record for the biggest striped bass ever caught on the island. Once I stopped being mad at Barry for not being Pop, I began to think he was okay.

Besides, since Barry had been around, Mom's eyes didn't have that sad, haunted look they'd had for so long after Pop died. I was grateful for that, even though it was kind of embarrassing to see a guy acting so big-time crazy about my mother.

Mom went on talking as she stirred onions and hamburger meat in the frying pan. "Yes, Ed told me you found it. *That* must have been a surprise."

She looked at me. My mouth was stuffed with cookies, so I just nodded.

"Well, anyway, the police found the owner and talked to him. Apparently, his son drove here from Connecticut for the weekend. I can't imagine letting a sixteen-year-old boy do that."

Big surprise. After Pop died, Mom had worried so much about something happening to me that she'd just about wrapped me in tissue paper and put me under her mattress for safekeeping. She was getting better, but I still figured I was going to be lucky if she ever let me drive around the block.

Judging from what Mom had just said, Donny had been right about the driver being a wealthy kid from off-island in his father's car. *Believe it, Daggett,* Donny had said. *And the rich kids who come here thinking they're better than us— they'd best believe it, too.* I wondered what that was supposed to mean. Jeff had acted as if he knew, sitting beside Donny and high-fiving him back.

I thought about how I'd reacted to seeing Jeff and Donny driving around together, and felt kind of embarrassed. What was I, a jealous girlfriend or something? But it was weird that Donny was hanging around with Jeff. Donny was sixteen. The three years' difference in our ages hadn't mattered so much when we were younger. I remembered a time when Jeff and I crashed one of his model planes out in the middle of Menemsha Pond. We didn't have a dinghy or any way to get it, and we were too little and too scared to swim. Donny swam out, got the plane, and brought it back in his mouth like a dog retrieving a stick. He even came over to us and pretended to wag his tail, then shook like a dog when he dropped the plane at our feet. I'd just about choked to death, I was laughing so hard.

I remembered another long, rainy afternoon at the Mannings' house when Donny had been there, too. We took Magic Markers and drew on all the faces in a deck of cards, and played stupid card games in which three-eyed jacks, kings with boogers, and queens with bad hair were wild.

Then there was the time a whole bunch of kids—boys, girls, all different ages—were at the beach in the summer. It was a really windy day, and I was flying a kite tied to the line on a fishing rod. Everybody was watching because the kite was flying so high. I was concentrating hard, both hands on the rod and both eyes on the little speck high in the air, when suddenly an older kid named Tony came up behind me and pulled my bathing suit down around my ankles.

Remembering it now, three years later, I could feel my face turning red with embarrassment all over again. I'd wanted to walk into the ocean and never come back to face all those kids—those *girls*—who had seen me naked.

But Donny had saved me. He threw a beach towel over

Tony's head, and said he was going to pull off Tony's suit unless he admitted that he was a creep for doing such a crummy thing.

"Say it!" Donny had demanded. "Admit you're a creep!" Everyone's attention turned to Donny and Tony, and Tony was the one who ended up looking like a dork.

Donny had seemed almost like a god to me that day. In a way, he still did. I decided I was making a big deal out of nothing. So Donny took Jeff for a ride in the Tomahawk. So maybe I wished Donny thought I was cool enough to go cruising around with him. So what? Get over it.

"Hey, Mom," I said, "can I go over to Jeff's after dinner?"

"*May* I go over to Jeff's," she corrected. Mom was a real grammar grouch.

"*May* I go to Jeff's?" I tried, along with my biggest, sweetest smile.

"Yes, but I want you home by nine-thirty. You've got a full day of work tomorrow."

"Okay."

We sat down to eat, and Mom continued talking about the car. "The odd thing is," she said, "that the boy who was driving never showed up to claim the car. He never reported it missing, either."

"I heard that," I said. "Boy, I bet he's in big trouble with his parents right now."

"Well, maybe," Mom answered, "except that right now, I imagine his parents are more worried than angry."

"They'll have plenty of time to get mad later, right, Mom?" I grinned at her, remembering when I'd sneaked out in the middle of the night during last year's fishing derby and scared Mom half to death. She sure hadn't thought it was funny at the time, but I figured maybe she could joke about it now.

"When he shows up, I hope they give him a big kiss and then ground him for the rest of his life," she said sternly.

I decided I didn't really want to know if she was kidding around or not. When we'd finished eating, I quickly cleared the dishes from the table, rinsed them in the sink, and headed for the door.

After calling good-bye to Mom, I pedaled up Lighthouse Road and coasted to a stop in the Mannings' driveway. Hearing laughter coming from the garage, I headed in that direction instead of toward the house. Soon I heard someone talking. The words stopped me in my tracks.

Four

"**IT WAS JUST TOO PERFECT,**" a voice said. "The stupid dork was stoned out of his mind. He left the car right on the boat ramp. All I did was let off the emergency brake. Maybe I gave it the smallest little push, you know what I'm saying?"

There was a laugh, and another voice mumbled something I couldn't understand. Then I heard more laughter.

The first voice said, "I figured it would roll a little and end up stuck in the sand. He'd have to get it towed, and it'd be a major pain in the tail. But that sucker kept right on going! I didn't mean to sink it, but, hey, it couldn't have happened to a nicer guy."

I recognized that first voice. It was Donny. And the other person was Jeff.

I stood frozen in place, my hands over my ears, not wanting to hear any more, not wanting to believe what I'd already heard. I wanted to run to my bike and ride away.

Instead, maybe just to stop the voices from saying anything more, I found myself calling, "Hey, Jeff, you in there?" I hadn't known I was going to do it, and I was amazed to hear how steady my voice sounded, how normal, even though I felt as though a big diesel engine was roaring through my head and chest.

There was a sudden hush from the garage, then Donny and Jeff stepped out. Jeff stared at the ground, but Donny looked right at me with narrowed eyes.

"How long have you been out here, Ben?" he asked. There was none of the usual fun or teasing in his expression.

"Not long," I answered quickly. "I heard you guys talking, so I was just coming—"

Donny interrupted. "What'd you hear?"

"Nothing," I said, holding up my empty hands as if to prove my innocence. I laughed, and to my own ears it sounded forced and phony. "Why? What's the big deal?"

Donny, too, was trying to act normal now, as if nothing out of the ordinary had happened. "No big deal," he said, giving me a little grin. To Jeff he said, "He's cool, right?"

"Yeah," answered Jeff. "He's cool."

Donny disappeared into the garage, and Jeff and I stood

uncomfortably in the driveway. He still hadn't met my eyes.

"What was *that* all about?" I asked.

"Nothing," he said, finally looking at me and giving a little shrug. "Donny was just messing around."

Jeff was lying to me; I couldn't believe it. Jeff was the one friend I'd always thought I could count on to tell me the real scoop. After Mom started dating Barry and I was really mad about it, Jeff had had the guts to say that maybe Barry was good for my mom. I hadn't wanted to hear it, but it sure made me think.

I decided to give him another chance to tell me what the heck was going on. "What's he doing in your garage?"

"Working on the Tomahawk," Jeff answered. "He needed to borrow some of my dad's tools."

I tried again. "Looks like you and Donny are big buddies all of a sudden. What do you guys talk about?"

"Nothing much."

Come off it, Jeff, I wanted to say. But I didn't. I felt off-balance from what I'd heard, and from the strange way Jeff was acting. I just stood there, sure he'd be able to read my thoughts on my face, but all he said was, "So, you want to see the airplane I got for my birthday? I've almost got it put together, but I still have to get the remote control rigged up."

I hesitated. Maybe if we worked on the plane together it would feel like old times, and Jeff would confide in me about what was going on with Donny. "Sure," I managed to say, and followed him inside, where Mr. and Mrs. Manning were watching television in the den.

Somehow I managed to say hello and answer their friendly, interested questions about my first day mating for Chick. Then I followed Jeff up to his room. We sat down at the card table he'd set up in the middle of the room, where the plane's assembly kit was spread out on sheets of waxed paper.

Jeff immediately began gluing a few final little pieces, holding them in place with pins, and talking nonstop about all the plane's special features. He was so into it that he didn't seem to notice anything odd about my behavior. Maybe I wasn't acting strange. But I sure felt weird.

Finally I couldn't stand it anymore. "Jeff," I said, "I heard you and Donny talking."

His hands stopped moving, and he looked up from the table. "Yeah, I thought so," he said with a little smile.

"Did Donny push that car into the harbor?"

Jeff looked at me. "What if he did?" he asked.

"Well, for cripe's sake, Jeff, *did he?*" I knew, but for some reason I wanted to hear Jeff say it.

"Yeah," Jeff said softly.

"But why?" I asked. "Is he crazy?" It came out more loudly than I'd expected.

Jeff looked nervously toward the door and whispered, "Shhh. Take it easy, Ben. He didn't mean to sink it."

"I can't believe it," I said, whispering now, too. "What if he gets caught?"

"He's not going to get caught." Jeff looked at me earnestly, really believing what he was saying.

"How do *you* know? The police are looking for the person who did it!"

Jeff shrugged. "Nobody saw him."

"But why did he do it?" I asked.

Jeff leaned toward me and said in a hushed voice, "You know Jen, Donny's girlfriend?"

I nodded. Everybody knew Jen and Donny.

"Well, the kid who was driving the car was hitting on Jen at South Beach the other day, trying to impress her with his fancy car, get her to go for a ride and stuff. So Donny was just, you know, teaching him a lesson."

"Geez," I said, imagining the whole scene. Donny was touchy about the Tomahawk, but that was nothing compared to how he was about Jen. No kid from the island would be brave—or stupid—enough to flirt with Jen since she'd started going out with Donny. Not that Donny went around threatening people or anything like that, but still, you didn't want Donny mad at you. You just never knew what he might do.

"So the kid had it coming," Jeff went on. "Maybe he'll tell his friends they can't just come here and throw their money around and treat us like dirt."

Treat *us* like dirt? What had the kid ever done to Jeff? I wondered. Then it hit me: *the kid!* "Where *is* the kid, anyway?" I asked.

Jeff shrugged again. "Don't know. I don't think anybody knows."

"Not even Donny?"

"Nope. Donny left after he pushed the car in, and he never saw the kid again after that."

"And the kid just let Donny push his car in the water?"

"No. He was out on the beach, meeting some other kids."

It was pretty clear that Jeff was taking Donny's side completely. He said, "You're not going to tell, are you?"

Tell? I hadn't thought that far ahead. When I didn't answer immediately, Jeff said, "*Ben.* You *can't* tell." He looked at me incredulously and urged, "Come *on*, Ben. It's not like he did it to one of *our* cars, like Chick's or your mom's or something. It belonged to one of *them*."

"That's why you're covering for him?"

"Well, yeah. What do I care about that rich little snot or his car? Donny's my *friend.*"

I couldn't even talk. My thoughts were too jumbled up, and Jeff seemed so sure.

"And *you're* my friend," he said. Then he added, "Right?"

"Well, duh."

He smiled, spreading his hands wide, as if that settled that.

I felt trapped in Jeff's small, cluttered bedroom. I couldn't breathe. Desperate to get away, I glanced at the clock. To my relief, it was almost nine-thirty. "Look, I really gotta go," I said, standing up. "You know how Mom is."

"Yeah," said Jeff. "Okay." Then, looking worried, he said, "You're not mad or anything?"

Mad? I didn't know what I was, but I wasn't mad at Jeff. I just needed time to think things over. "No," I said.

"Good," he answered, and flashed me his old smile.

I raced down the stairs, said a quick good-bye to the Mannings, and stepped out into the driveway. There was a light coming from the garage. Great. The last thing I wanted to do was run into Donny again. I crept toward my bike, trying not to let the gravel crunch beneath my feet.

"Leaving, Ben?" Donny seemed to materialize out of nowhere. Suddenly he was standing between my bike and me. His voice was casual and light, as usual.

"Yeah," I said, "and I've got to hurry. Mom'll kill me if I'm late."

Donny smiled his lazy smile, but his eyes seemed to be sizing me up. "Hey, you remember when I found out about your secret cave?" he asked.

"Yes," I said, puzzled. It wasn't at all what I'd expected him to say.

Jeff and I had discovered a cave up in the clay cliffs, and for about four years now, it had been our secret place. We kept sleeping bags, rods, reels, and lures there, and matches and driftwood for campfires. We'd had some of our best times in that cave. Something that made it even cooler was that I had discovered my father's initials, JUD, for Jack Ulysses Daggett, carved into the clay on the back wall. Pop told me it had been his secret place when he was a kid. Jeff's initials and mine were carved right next to Pop's.

One day when Jeff and I were slipping through the narrow entrance to the cave, I looked back and saw Donny watching us. Later, he told me he wouldn't tell anybody, and as far as I knew, he'd kept his promise.

"I never told anybody your little secret, you know."

"I know, Donny," I said, trying to smile. "Thanks." I started to go, but Donny reached out and touched my arm, and I turned back to face him.

"And I never will tell, Ben," he said very slowly, emphasizing each word. "You can count on me."

"That's great, Donny. Thanks."

Donny grinned and gave me a soft punch on the shoulder. "Jeff said you were cool. How about we pick you up in the Tomahawk tomorrow night before the fireworks?"

I was so surprised, my jaw dropped. Donny wanted me to go with him to the fireworks? I quickly closed my mouth, then managed to stammer, "Well, yeah, sure. I mean, that'd be great."

"Around eight?"

"Yeah, sure."

"We'll have us a *party!*" he said, then added with a wink, "Better get going. You don't want your mom to ground you."

I stood for a moment, watching Donny walk back to the garage, before I got on my bike and began racing down the hill. The beam of the Aquinnah lighthouse flashed red-white-red-white-red-white across the sky. Usually the familiar light was a comforting sign that all was well, but no matter how hard I pumped my legs, I couldn't escape the feeling that tonight it was sending me a warning.

Five

BARRY'S CAR WAS in the driveway when I got home. I lingered outside for a minute, trying to collect my wildly spinning thoughts. Somehow, without exactly meaning to, I had promised not to tell about Donny and the Porsche. Donny had invited me to go with him to the fireworks the following night and, somehow, I had agreed that he would pick me up at eight o'clock.

Mom would not approve of any of this, I was sure. But the opportunity to arrive at Oak Bluffs for the big Fourth of July celebration in style, in the Tomahawk, with Donny, was too good to pass up. I'd been so dumbfounded when he asked me—okay, I admitted to myself, I'd been so *flattered*—that I couldn't say no. I couldn't look at Donny and say, "My mom won't let me." I'd feel like a total weenie. Especially since Jeff was going.

So I had to figure a way to get out of the house without Mom knowing I was going out with Donny. And now I had to go inside and act normal, or Mom's radar would pick up right away that something had happened tonight.

I took a deep breath and opened the front door. Mom called, "Ben? Is that you?"

"Hi," I said, walking into the living room, where she and Barry were sitting.

"How are you, Ben?" said Barry. "I hear you made quite an interesting discovery."

For one panicked second I thought he knew I had discovered that Donny had sunk the Porsche. But then I realized he was talking about me being the one to find it.

"Yeah," I said. "Good thing it wasn't one of your rentals, huh?"

Barry laughed. "People have done a lot of stupid things to my cars, but nobody's sunk one—yet."

"Tell Ben what you were just telling me," Mom urged Barry. Mom tended to be kind of a cheerleader when it came to Barry and me, always trying to keep the conversation going between us. I'd told her to relax, that Barry and I were fine with each other and she didn't have to worry about it. But sometimes she couldn't help herself, I guess.

I sat down, glad to have Mom's focus on Barry and not me.

Barry began, "Well, tonight I rented a car to the parents of the boy who was driving the Porsche. The Maddoxes. They flew in this evening because their son Cameron still hasn't turned up."

"Really?" I asked, definitely interested now. So the kid's name was Cameron Maddox.

"It's so peculiar," Mom said. "Where do you suppose he's hiding? And why?"

I could think of plenty of places to hide in the miles of forest and sandy dunes and hidden coves and inlets around the island. As for *why* he was hiding, I had a pretty good idea about that, too.

Now that I knew the story about this Cameron guy flirting with Jen, I thought it was possible he was hiding from *Donny.* Or, maybe after seeing what happened to his car, he'd gotten Donny's message loud and clear, and left the island on the next ferry. But that wasn't what I said to Mom and Barry.

"Don't you think he's embarrassed that his car ended up in the ocean?" I asked. "He's probably not exactly looking forward to seeing his parents. 'Hi, Mom and Dad.

Hope you don't mind that I ruined your zillion-dollar sports car.'"

"True," Barry agreed. "Mr. Maddox was rather intimidating."

"How so?" asked Mom.

Barry was silent for a minute, as if choosing his words. "It struck me that he seemed less interested in finding his son than in blaming someone for the kid's disappearance. He's convinced the police know something and are covering it up."

"That's ridiculous," Mom protested.

"I know. I tried to tell him that, but he more or less told me to shut my mouth, mind my own business, and rent him a car."

Mom shook her head.

"What a jerk," I said. It was one thing that *I* used to bad-mouth Barry; it made me really mad to think of this Maddox guy doing it.

"I told myself the man is under a lot of stress, with his son missing and all," said Barry.

"Still, there's no excuse for being rude," Mom replied.

"I figure Cameron will show up soon," said Barry. "When he's hungry and thirsty enough, or"—he gave a short laugh—"when he runs out of money."

"I hope you're right," said Mom. Then she turned to me. "What time are you meeting Chick in the morning?"

"Six-thirty."

"Hadn't you better turn in? It's almost ten."

For once I didn't argue. I said good night and got ready for bed. I worried that I might toss and turn all night, thinking about Donny and Cameron Maddox and how I was going to get out of the house to go to the fireworks, but I must have been more tired than I realized. Anyway, before I knew it, the alarm was ringing and it was time to go fishing again.

Six

I **DIDN'T COMPLETELY WAKE UP** until I was on the road to West Basin, with the sun warming my face and lighting up the dune grass, and shining through the mist that rose from the salt marshes. Hardly anyone was out and about except fishermen, who were either coming in from a night of surf casting off the beach or preparing to head out in their boats. It was a time of day Pop and I used to share, and in those early morning moments, it was easy to imagine that he was still close by.

Chick passed me in his blue pickup and waved. Soon I pulled into the parking area and chained and padlocked my bike to his rear bumper. By five minutes to seven, we were ready and waiting for our charter to arrive. At seven-fifteen, we were still waiting. By seven twenty-five, Chick was checking his watch every three seconds and muttering impatiently under his breath.

I knew how he felt. If our charter didn't show up, he was out a whole day's pay. If they showed up late, there was a good chance somebody else would have beaten us to the spot where Chick wanted to go, and we'd have to work that much harder to find fish and catch them.

We waited, watching other boats leaving the harbor one by one. At ten minutes of eight, Chick was just about to pack it in, when a brand-new Jeep sped into the lot, then a guy and a girl got out. I wasn't so good at telling people's ages, but it seemed to me that they were somewhere in their twenties.

They were both really good looking. I mean, I was no expert on guys' looks, but even I could see this was the kind of guy a lot of girls went nuts over. I admit I didn't spend a whole lot of time checking him out because she was, as Donny would say, a major babe. I'm talking about looks that don't seem real, as if she'd stepped out of a movie or the pages of a magazine or something.

I was just standing there, staring like an idiot, as they began walking toward us, but Chick called to them, "I wouldn't park there."

The guy turned back toward his Jeep. There, in plain sight, was a sign that said, PERMIT PARKING ONLY. Five spots were reserved for the harbormaster, the shellfish

41

warden, and a few charter-boat captains who had paid for permits. The guy shrugged and kept on walking toward us.

"You'll get a ticket," said Chick.

"Whatever," said the guy carelessly. "It's ridiculous. You can't park anywhere on this stupid island."

It was an annoying comment, made more so by the fact that there were half a dozen open spaces not twenty feet from the guy's Jeep. He wasn't entirely wrong, though. Once the summer season started, the narrow, winding roads of the Vineyard were overrun with more cars than they could handle, and parking became a nightmare, not just for tourists, but for everybody.

Chick turned away, muttering to himself, "Suit yourself, buddy."

"You know the car they found in the water?" the guy went on. He acted as though he was talking to his girl-friend, but he spoke loud enough for us to hear. "I figure the owner gave up and pushed it in because he couldn't find a place to park it."

He laughed, and the girl laughed, too, punching his arm and saying, "You're terrible."

I looked at Chick, rolled my eyes, and muttered, "Ha ha."

The guy came closer and said, "So you're Chick?"

Chick turned back around. "Yes," he answered evenly.

"Oh." The guy sounded disappointed. "I was hoping your boat would be bigger." He frowned, looking the *Something Fishy* over. Turning to the girl, he said, "What do you think?"

With a sinking feeling, I realized that this guy and his girlfriend or wife, or whoever she was, were our charter for the day. I didn't dare look at Chick. Like most of the captains I knew, he took a lot of pride in his boat. Chick kept the *Something Fishy* clean and in great shape, and it was plenty big enough for this guy and his girlfriend to fish from comfortably.

The girl looked at Chick and flashed a flirtatious smile. "I only care about one thing," she said. "Does it have a bathroom?"

"The head's up there," said Chick, pointing under the bow.

"Can I look?" She smiled like a naughty little girl when she said this.

Chick shrugged and said, "Be my guest."

The girl ignored the towel Chick had spread on the dock for wiping feet, and stepped into the boat. The treads of her sneakers left clumps of wet sand with each step as she moved to the bow, bent over, and peered through the forward hatch. She stayed that way for a long time, as if she was posing for a picture in her teeny little sweater and tight, low-cut jeans. I had the feeling she knew exactly how she looked and that she knew we were watching. I turned away.

"Well," she said, glancing up at the guy and shrugging delicately, "I guess I can rough it."

That really bugged me. The head in the *Something Fishy* was nice, roomier than the ones in most other boats and spotlessly clean, thanks to me. What the heck did she expect?

The guy laughed and, without a word to Chick or me, thrust a cooler he'd brought from the Jeep into my hands. I took it, and bent to stow it where it wouldn't bounce and slide around when we were running.

"Just a second there," Chick said. I looked up when I heard the sharp tone of his voice, very different from his usual friendly, laid-back way of speaking. He was staring right at the guy, his hands hanging loosely by his sides. He appeared relaxed. But from the tight set of his jaw and the narrow squint of his eyes, I knew that Chick didn't much like this guy and was about to set him straight.

"Am I to assume you're my charter for today?"

The guy made a face that implied Chick was the stupidest person he'd ever met. "Well, yeah. What'd you think?"

"I think you're late," said Chick.

Now I knew Chick was PO'd. He was basically pretty

easy-going, and was always polite to clients. Unless they really provoked him. *Way to go, Chick,* I thought.

"Yeah, I know you said seven," said the guy. "But I figured that meant, you know, *around* seven." He grinned, and jerked his thumb toward the girl. "You know how tough it is to get chicks moving in the morning. The hair, the makeup, the clothes. You're lucky we showed up before noon."

"*You're* lucky we're still here," said Chick. There was a pause, and I waited tensely to see if this was going to turn into a real argument. Then Chick said, "But since we are, let's go fishing." He put out his hand. "I'm Captain Chick Flanders, and this is my first mate, Ben Daggett."

I felt myself start to relax. Chick was going to try to lighten things up. The guy stared at Chick for a moment before taking his hand. "Brad Gibbons," he said finally, ignoring me.

The girl stepped up and took Chick's hand next. "Nicole Ford," she said. "But you can call me Nicki."

Chick nodded briefly. "Okay. Let's go."

Brad stepped into the boat. I sighed as I noticed that his shoes had black rubber treads. I'd be spending a good half hour that afternoon scrubbing stubborn black scuff marks off the deck.

Chick had heard that the bonito and false albacore were

feeding right outside the jetties at the mouth of Menemsha harbor. We still had gas from the day before, so we headed through the channel into the open sound. Sure enough, we could see places where the surface of the water was boiling. The commotion was made by hundreds of lightning-quick fish called bonito swimming hungrily through schools of panicked little sand eels. The air was filled with the shrieks of terns and gulls as they hovered over the frenzy, then dipped down to grab the wounded bait fish left behind after each blitz.

To me, there was nothing more exciting than casting into a group of fish feeding at the surface like that. But we were too late to get near them. Twelve other boats encircled the feeding fish. Fishermen, just as agitated as the fish and birds, threw lures at the seething water. Chick pulled up outside the ring of boats and put the engine in neutral while we watched one guy hook up, then another.

Brad turned to Chick and said impatiently, "What are we waiting for?"

"Pretty exciting, huh?" said Chick, still watching the action and smiling. "But I'm not going to crowd those guys," he explained. "They got here first."

"So?" asked Brad. "I thought we came out here to catch fish. That's what I'm paying you for."

I watched Chick take a deep breath before he answered. I was thinking it was a good thing I wasn't the captain because I'd be tempted to tell Brad off. "Those guys got out here bright and early and got the jump on us," Chick said. "We'll find some other fish."

Watching the effort Chick was making to control his anger, I tried to do the same. It was easy for Brad to say we should horn in on the action by the jetty. He had just breezed onto the island for a few days of sun and fun, while we lived here year-round. Many of those guys were our friends and neighbors, and there were some things you just didn't do when you were fishing. It wasn't that there were rules, exactly. It was like anything else: you went by common sense and courtesy. Two things Brad didn't seem to be overflowing with, I thought, getting mad all over again.

Chick put the engine in forward and said to me, "We'll check out the bar and see if there's anything going on. If not, we'll work our way up around the cliffs."

I nodded. We ran the shoreline toward the big sand spit known as Dogfish Bar. It was a calm morning, and the sun was already beginning to warm the air. It was going to be a beautiful day. I hoped Brad would loosen up and enjoy it.

There was nothing doing at the bar, so we moved on to work the rocks at Devil's Bridge. No fish showed on the surface, but Chick said he wanted to try drifting the rocks for bass. "Do you want to spin cast or fish with bait?" he asked.

Brad reached for one of the spinning rods. Nicki, already looking bored, said, "Whatever."

Chick told me to rig up a bait rod for her. I was slipping a chunk of mackerel on the hook, when Brad cursed loudly, adding, "Cheap piece of junk rod!"

He had tried to cast a lure, but instead of sailing out in the direction he intended, it dropped onto the deck behind him. That was not the rod's fault, but Brad's. He had released his thumb from the spool too early in the cast. Lots of people who weren't used to fishing did that before they got their rhythm. It wasn't anything to make a big deal about.

Chick and I looked at each other, then turned back to what we were doing without saying anything. From the corner of my eye, I watched Brad cast again. That time he released too late, and the lure landed with a loud splat in the water two feet from the side of the boat.

Swearing more under his breath, he tried again. The lure landed a decent distance away, but instead of retrieving it, he seemed to be struggling with the reel.

I saw the problem: he was holding the rod upside down and reeling backward. "It works different from a bait-casting reel," I said. "Turn it over. Like this." I demonstrated with the rod I held in my hand.

"I always do it this way," said Brad.

I shrugged and turned back to the rod I was rigging. I

felt like laughing out loud, but I knew it would only make the situation worse.

Finally, Brad turned the rod right side up and began reeling, but by then his lure had sunk too deep and gotten hooked on a rock. He hauled back and yanked hard on the rod.

"Take it easy, there," said Chick. "Let out some slack and I'll—"

But at that moment Brad jerked again and the line snapped. With an exclamation of disgust, he threw the rod onto the deck and said, "I need a beer."

Chick picked up the rod and checked it for damage. From where I was, I could see that one of the eyes had broken off.

Nicki reached into the cooler, handed Brad a can of beer, and took one for herself. He said to her, plenty loud enough for Chick and me to hear, "There's no fish here, anyway."

Yeah, right, I thought furiously. *A lot you know.* Pop had caught the biggest striped bass ever recorded on the island right here at Devil's Bridge. And during the fishing derby last fall, casting from the beach toward this very spot, I had caught my big one. I was about to say something when Chick caught my eye, nodded toward the rod I was holding, and picked up a spinning rod himself.

Hiding my grin, I let down the hook baited with

mackerel and waited, while Chick threw out a heavy, silver bucktail jig. After a few casts, Chick pulled in a nice striper. Without a word to Brad, he removed the hook and released the fish. A few seconds later, I felt a tug on the end of my line. I, too, had a fish. Following Chick's lead, I unhooked mine and watched it swim away.

Figuring, I guess, that we'd made our point, Chick said casually, "So, are you guys going to fish or what?"

"I'm going to catch some rays," said Nicki, stepping out of her jeans and pulling her sweater over her head. In her bikini, beer in hand, she spread out on the bow with her face to the sun.

"This spot stinks," said Brad, chugging down the rest of his beer and opening another. "Let's find some decent-sized fish."

I watched the muscles in Chick's jaw twitch. Ignoring Brad's comment, he said, "Ben, why don't you get the trolling rods out."

"Sure thing," I said, thinking, *Smart idea.* If we trolled, there was still a chance for a successful day. We'd run at slow speed, with four rods set off the stern, dragging the lures along behind us. That way Brad's lack of casting skill wouldn't matter. The forward movement of the boat more or less hooked the fish, and all Brad would have to do was reel them in. At least we wouldn't have to listen to his tantrums and excuses.

We trolled for about an hour. Chick and I watched the rods, and Brad joined Nicki on the bow, where they drank one beer after another. Since the bow was raised, separated from the rest of the boat by a windshield in front of the console, we couldn't hear them talking over the hum of the engine, and that was fine with us.

"I'd rather clean up after a barfing kid any day," I murmured. "That guy is really getting on my nerves."

"Hang in there, Ben. It'll soon be over."

But it got a lot worse before it was over.

Seven

SEVERAL MINUTES LATER, Nicki climbed down from the bow, announcing with a giggle, "Gotta pee." Unsteady from the beers she had drunk, she teetered on the gunwale and grabbed the radio antenna to balance herself. The antenna snapped off in her hand. Chick caught her in time to keep her from going overboard, but the antenna fell from her fingers and quickly sank from sight.

Without a thank-you to Chick for helping her or an apology for the broken antenna, she disappeared into the head. After she emerged, she rummaged through her backpack, removed a small leather case, and took it onto the bow with her. Taking a cigarette from the case, she lit it, took a deep drag, and handed it over to Brad. He, too, inhaled deeply. A sweet, pungent odor drifted back to Chick and me.

"What the—?" I looked at Chick, whose face was flushed a deep, angry red. "Take the wheel," he said. He leaned around the windshield and said in a low voice, "Get rid of that."

Brad looked up, took another drag from the cigarette, and held it out to Chick. "Want a hit, Cap?"

"Throw it overboard," Chick said emphatically. "Now."

"What's the big deal?" Brad said lazily. "There's nobody around but us chickens." He seemed to think that was pretty funny, and laughed until he choked a little on the smoke he was exhaling.

"I said throw it over," said Chick.

Nicki sat up then and said, "Aw, lighten up, Captain Chick. C'mon, join us."

"Listen," said Chick, his voice tight and furious. "If we get busted with that stuff on board, I can lose my license and my boat."

I had been watching and listening to the conversation, trying to figure out what Chick was so upset about. Now I knew. Brad and Nicki were smoking *dope*. I felt stupid not to have figured it out before. I knew kids from school who used drugs, but I'd never been around when they were doing it. We'd all been shown what marijuana looked like in the drug awareness program at school, touched it and sniffed it and all that, but it was different when it was lit. It smelled kind of like burning rope mixed with incense.

The thing was, the Coast Guard had gotten really serious about stopping drug traffic. They'd started a "Zero Tolerance" policy, which meant that they could seize any boat that had drugs on board, even if the captain didn't know anything about them. It didn't seem fair that Chick could get punished for what somebody like Brad did, but that was the way it was.

Brad swept his arm across the empty horizon. "Who's going to bust us? Do you see any cops out here? Do you see *anybody* out here?" Looking at Nicki, he said, "I sure don't see any *fish* out here." That really cracked him up, and he began laughing again.

Chick wasn't laughing. In one swift motion, he swung himself up onto the bow, reached down, grabbed the cigarette from Brad's hand, and threw it into the water. "Is there more in there?" he demanded, pointing to Nicki's little leather case.

She clutched the case to her chest and didn't answer.

"Is there?"

"That's none of your business, pal," said Brad, rising to his feet.

Brad and Chick stood face to face, glowering at each

other. "It's my boat, and that makes it my business," said Chick. "Either she throws it out now, or I get on the radio and report this. Coast Guard headquarters are right in Menemsha, and they'd be happy to meet us at the dock."

There was a silence that seemed to go on forever. I didn't know whether Chick was too mad to remember that the radio antenna was broken, or if he was bluffing, counting on Brad and Nicki to be too stupid to realize it. It didn't much matter; Chick could still head right into Coast Guard headquarters if he wanted to.

Finally, Brad reached down and took the leather case from Nicki. Without taking his eyes from Chick's face, he unzipped the case and took out a small plastic bag. "You know how much this is worth, man?" he asked.

Chick shrugged. "I don't know and I don't care."

With an expression of utter disgust, Brad tossed the bag into the water. "Happy now, Captain Blowfish?" he asked.

Chick turned away. He swung back down onto the center deck and said tersely, "Party's over."

Leaving the engine running at trolling speed, we reeled in the lines and stowed all the gear. Chick took the wheel and called over the windshield, "You'll want to come down from there. It's going to be a rough, wet ride heading back."

Nicki looked at Brad, who stared back at Chick without saying a word.

"Fine," said Chick under his breath. "Stay there." He pushed the throttle forward, and the *Something Fishy* responded with a surge of power. Brad and Nicki scrambled to hold on to the railing around the edge of the bow.

On the return trip, Chick made no effort to ease up at the approach of big waves or patches of rough water. I had to admit, I enjoyed the sight of Brad and Nicki trying to look nonchalant and in control as they thudded and bounced about, getting soaked by wave after wave breaking over the bow.

It was a little before noon when we pulled into West Basin. Nicki and Brad scrambled off the bow onto the dock. Brad reached into his wallet, removed a couple of bills, and held them out to Chick. "That's half. Not that you deserve it."

Chick kept his hands at his sides. "Keep it," he said, and turned away.

I stared at Brad, wanting so badly to say what I thought of him. He smirked at me, and said to Nicki, "What a joke. Come on; let's go."

Neither Chick nor I turned to look as Brad sped away, his Jeep's tires squealing in the parking lot.

I slammed my fist on the console. "That snot-faced jerk! Why didn't you take his money? You should have made him pay for a whole day! It's his fault we came in early."

"Forget it, Ben," Chick said quietly. "Every once in a

while you get a loser like that guy. You can't let 'em get to you."

"Are you kidding?" I said, almost shouting. "I felt like punching his lights out! He loses a perfectly good lure, busts your rod, his drunken girlfriend snaps off the antenna, and he doesn't even offer to pay for them!"

"Take it easy, Ben. I don't want his money."

But I wasn't finished. "Then he has the nerve to say you don't know where the fish are, when we're fishing at Devil's Bridge, for cripe's sake! Captain Blowfish, he called you, the big, fat"—I shook my head in disgust, unable to think of a word for Brad that wouldn't get me in trouble with Chick, who didn't like swearing—"barnacle butt!"

I saw the faintest smile cross Chick's face.

"And how about when he was reeling backward and tried to tell me, 'I always do it this way.' "

At that, Chick began to laugh. "I could barely keep a straight face when he came out with that one."

"Unbelievable!" I said, still furious.

"But I have to say," Chick said, laughing harder now, "I kind of enjoyed the ride home, didn't you?"

I had to smile at the memory of Brad flying around on the bow, sopping wet. "Funny how you kept hitting those waves dead on," I said.

"What do you mean?" Chick asked innocently. "I always do it that way."

That cracked me up. We joked for a while more about Brad and Nicki while we cleaned up the boat, and it felt good to blow off steam.

But soon the anger rose in me again. Maybe Jeff was right: there was *us* and there was *them*. "Chick, doesn't it make you mad? Who does that puke-brain think he is, coming here and treating us like dirt?"

Chick sighed. "He's one of the ones I warned you about, Ben. When it comes to tourists, you take the bad with the good. Without them, I wouldn't have a job and neither would you. Neither would your mom, or Barry, or more than half the people you know."

"I know, but—"

"Just hear me out for a second," Chick said. "Guys like Brad are like sand flies. They're annoying. You've got to learn to brush 'em off." His hand brushed away an imaginary fly. "Every job has its hassles. But if you want to eat, you've got to work, and I'm willing to work hard to earn my money." He stopped and looked at me meaningfully. "Still, there are things that are more valuable than money, Ben. Like self-respect.

"I'll put up with a guy like Brad until he crosses the line. My line. Nobody can treat me like dirt if I don't let him. Do you understand what I'm saying?"

"I guess," I answered, even though I wasn't really sure I

did. "But, Chick, because of him, you're out a whole day's pay. Worse, because you burned up fuel and stuff taking him out for nothing."

Chick shrugged. "I'll tell you what would really be worse. If we were still out there with that gas bag." He looked at me and smiled. "True?"

I smiled back. "True."

"What would be worse is if I wanted his money so badly I was willing to put up with him to get it." Chick reached into his pocket and held out my thirty dollars' pay. "Now go to the beach, have a swim, and forget about Brad."

"No," I said, pushing the money back.

"Come on, take it. Just because I didn't want that kid's money doesn't mean I'm going to stiff you."

"Forget it, Chick," I said. "You don't get paid, I don't get paid. That's *my* line, and you can't cross it." I gave him a smug look, daring him to try to talk his way out of that one.

He laughed. "Well, that sure came back to bite me in the rear, didn't it? Okay, Ben, you win. I'll see you tomorrow."

"Who have we got tomorrow?" I asked cautiously.

"An old client of mine and his son. Nice guy."

"If you say so."

I didn't have time to worry about tomorrow's clients, anyway. I was still ticked off about Brad and Nicki, and I had another problem on my mind, too.

Somehow, I had to get out of the house to meet Donny without letting Mom know where I was going or whom I was going with.

Eight

SINCE CHICK AND I had come in early, I had a couple of hours before Mom got home to think about what I was going to tell her. The thing was, Mom and I had come to a sort of understanding after I'd run away during the derby last year. She said she'd try to loosen up and stop worrying all the time that something was going to happen to me, and I said I'd try to let her know where I was and what I was doing and not make her worry.

So far we'd both been doing pretty well. But Mom would never understand why I wanted to go to the fireworks with Donny. She'd say if I wanted to go to the fireworks, she and Barry would take me, which wouldn't be the same thing at all. She'd talk about the accident rate for sixteen-year-old boys driving cars, and she'd ask why

Donny was all of a sudden asking me to go places with him.

Which was maybe a good question, but the fact was, Donny did invite me, and I wanted to go. If I didn't, Donny and Jeff would go without me, and Donny probably would never ask me again.

Maybe it's a basic rule of life that mothers don't care about the same things kids care about. For example, Mom would never understand why I wanted to go out with Donny for a couple of hours just one night, have a little fun, maybe be seen in the Tomahawk by some of the kids from school.

I argued with her in my head: *But Jeff's going.* Of course, I was pretty sure Jeff's parents didn't know the whole story. But, really, what was the big deal?

I called Jeff. "Hi," I said. "Are you going with Donny tonight?"

"Yeah. Are you coming?"

"I'm trying to figure out what to tell my mom."

"Tell her what I told mine: Chick's taking us."

I thought about it. It could work. Mom certainly trusted Chick, and she wasn't likely to call him and check.

"But what about when Donny comes to pick you up?"

"I told him I'd be at your house."

"Brilliant move, Jeff!"

"It was kind of dumb," he admitted. "But it was all I could think of at the time."

"I know!" I said. "Call him and tell him to pick us up at the corner of Lighthouse and Lobsterville Roads. You tell your parents you're coming to my house and getting a ride with Chick from here, and I'll say I'm getting picked up at your house. We'll meet halfway, ditch our bikes in the bushes, and wait for Donny."

"Okay," Jeff agreed. "Sounds good. I hope I can get hold of Donny, though. I think he's working at that garage in Vineyard Haven today."

"Well, try."

"All right. Hey, about last night? You didn't say anything, did you?"

"No," I said. "And don't worry. I won't. After today, there's a Jeep I wouldn't mind pushing into the ocean."

"What?"

"I'll tell you later."

After a few minutes, Jeff called back to say the plan was a go.

The trouble with a guilty conscience is that you can't relax. I was jumpy all afternoon, waiting for Mom to get home. When she did, she called up the stairs, "Benjamin Daggett? Come down here right now, please."

It was her no-nonsense voice. Uh-oh. I hurried downstairs, sure she had already found out about my intended treachery. I could feel my face flaming. When I walked into the kitchen, Mom was putting away groceries, her back to me.

"Yes?" I said, knowing it drove her crazy when I said "Yeah."

She turned around and pointed to the table, where I had left my dirty lunch dishes. "Ben, how many times have I asked you to clean up after yourself? You know the problems we've had with ants."

Whew. I let out my breath slowly. "Sorry, Mom," I said, carrying the dishes to the sink and washing them. "I was kind of distracted when I got home today. Chick and I came in at noon."

"Really?" Mom asked. "What happened?"

"We had some obnoxious clients."

Mom made a face. "It must be going around. I had a gentleman—and I use the term loosely—give me a hard time today because he left his garbage out uncovered, and skunks got into it. He was furious that the trash collectors didn't pick it up, even though it was strewn all over the place. I honestly think he expected me to come clean it up for him!"

I shook my head in sympathy.

"What happened with you and Chick?" she asked.

"Well, this guy and his girlfriend were really rude, but the reason we came in was they started smoking pot. Chick threw it overboard and then refused to take their money."

"Good for him," Mom said. She sighed and added, "This summer is the worst I can remember, and it's only just started. I suppose you heard about the robbery last night?"

"No," I said. "What robbery?"

"I assumed everybody at Squid Row would be buzzing about it."

"We didn't go over to the gas dock today," I said. "What happened?"

"Somebody broke into one of the big cabin cruisers and took cigarettes, liquor, and some expensive fishing equipment. The owner and his wife were out to dinner, I guess. They got back about midnight, discovered what had happened, and called Pete. He's completely mystified."

So was I. In all the years Pop had fished out of the Menemsha docks, he'd never had one thing stolen off his boat. No one I knew ever had. It was just the way it was: no one touched a fisherman's boat. Or anybody else's.

"Must have been a tourist," I said. "Nobody from around here would do that."

"That's what Pete said," Mom replied. "Probably who- ever did it left on the ferry and is long gone by now. It's the kind of case the police might never solve."

Barry came over after a while, and cooked us some bluefish a friend of his had caught. While we ate, he told us about a woman who had come into the agency early that morning.

"She wanted a Jeep or a beach buggy so she could go out to Wasque to fish the beach," he said. "I told her I was sorry, that all my off-road vehicles were already out, and suggested places where she could fish without running the beach. I thought she was satisfied, because she rented a regular car.

"Well, round about four, four-thirty this afternoon, she called from her cell phone. And guess where she was?"

I could guess, but I hated when people blew my punch lines and I wanted to hear Barry tell it. "Where?" I asked.

"Stuck up to her rims out at Wasque and madder than all get-out—at *me*!" Barry laughed incredulously and shook his head. "She ordered me to come get her right away and said she expected every penny of her money back."

"No way!" I said. "What did you do?"

"I told her I'd be happy to send a tow truck to pull her out, but that she'd be responsible for paying for it. Then I very politely reminded her that her rental agreement specifically prohibited off-road use and that she would also be responsible for any damage to the car."

"What did she say to that?" Mom asked.

"Oh, lots," said Barry with a little chuckle. "But when she was finished, I simply asked, 'So, do you want me to send a tow truck or not?' And I mentioned that if she got back in after midnight, she'd be charged for another day."

"Nice touch," I said.

Barry grinned.

"Summer truly has begun," said Mom with a sigh. "Ben, tell Barry about what happened out on the boat today."

I told the story of Brad and Nicki again, complete with all the gory details. Mom and Barry made a pretty good audience, with Mom shaking her head and *tsk-tsk*ing at some of Brad's remarks, and Barry rolling his eyes in exasperation.

After I got to the part about the dope, Mom said, "Oh, speaking of that, the word around the office today was that Cameron Maddox—you know, the missing boy—"

I broke in to ask, "He hasn't shown up yet?"

"No," said Mom. "The police have reason to believe he was here on the island selling drugs and that his disappearance might be related to that. His parents claim that's ridiculous, but . . . " Her voice trailed off, and she shrugged. "I guess we'll find out. Anyway, enough of these upsetting subjects. The fireworks are tonight. Who feels like going?"

Here goes, I thought. I took a deep breath and explained the plan.

"Oh, how nice of Chick to take you boys," Mom said. "Barry, do you feel like going?"

"I will if you want to, Kate, but, to tell you the truth, the last thing I feel like doing is going back down-island and dealing with all that traffic."

"That's fine with me," said Mom. "I'm pretty tired, and you know they never start the show until after ten o'clock. Ben, I'm sure Chick will bring you right home after, won't he? He has to get up early, too."

I nodded. Mom began clearing the table, and I jumped up to help. I couldn't believe it had been that easy. And I didn't even have to worry about Mom and Barry seeing me in town with Donny. When the dishes were done, I announced that I was going to Jeff's to meet Chick.

"Okay, sweetie," Mom said, giving me a kiss. "Have fun."

Barry called good-bye from the living room. "Need money for junk food?" he asked.

"Nope," I called back. "Thanks."

Biking up the road, I felt like a real creep, lying to Mom and Barry that way. If only they had given me a hard time,

I'd be able to feel more justified in deceiving them. But they'd been so nice, so trusting, so unsuspecting.

Have fun.

Need any money?

Geez.

I tried to shake off the guilty feeling and get psyched up for the evening ahead. It was going to be great, I told myself, well worth the cost of a harmless little lie.

Nine

WHEN DONNY PULLED UP to the corner where Jeff and I were waiting, music boomed from the Tomahawk's open windows. Donny motioned for us to get in, and Jeff, with a smug glance in my direction, hopped into the front seat. I climbed into the back, where I could feel the rear speakers pounding in my ears and thumping in my chest.

Donny said something to Jeff that I couldn't hear over the music. "What?" I shouted.

Donny turned down the volume a little bit. "I've got to make a stop on the way," I heard him saying, "but we've got lots of time before the fireworks start. You know how they always drag it out, waiting for people to spend all their money on food and stuff."

"No problem," said Jeff. "Where's Jen?"

I admired the easy way he asked the question, as if he and Donny and Jen were old buddies. I was feeling kind of tongue-tied, not wanting to say or do anything that would make Donny regret asking me to come along.

"Her family's got company for the weekend, and she has to go to the fireworks with them. So this is boys' night out," Donny answered, meeting my eyes in the rearview mirror and giving me his knowing grin.

We cruised down-island, not talking much after that. Well, Donny and Jeff said a few things to each other, but it was just about impossible to hear them over the music, which was still really loud, and after a while I gave up. Jeff turned to me a few times and smiled, looking happy and excited. I was pretty excited, too.

Donny turned off the main road near the airport, onto an unpaved road, then onto a smaller road that was little more than a narrow, sandy path. We bounced along, passing a few houses. Then for a while there was nothing but scrubby oak trees, beach plums, and giant poison ivy plants that brushed the sides of the Tomahawk. The road ended at a little house set off by itself in the dense undergrowth. There was a dilapidated old wooden boat up on blocks sitting in the yard, along with some car parts, a few busted-up lobster pots, a rusted chair, and a jumble of assorted tools and other junk.

Donny jumped out, leaving his door open and the radio on. He went around behind the Tomahawk and reached into the trunk. A skinny little guy with a long, greasy-looking gray ponytail appeared at the door of the house, glared at Jeff and me, and disappeared back inside. He looked vaguely familiar, and after a second I placed him: he was the guy who had honked at us when I'd been standing in the road talking to Donny and Jeff in the Tomahawk.

Jeff and I watched Donny pick his way carefully through the yard to the door, carrying what looked like three heavy-duty, open-ocean fishing rods with big, gold-tone reels.

"Look at those Penn Internationals!" I shouted to Jeff.

"Yeah," he said admiringly. "I wonder where he got them? They're worth—what? Like five hundred dollars apiece?"

"More like a thousand, I think," I answered.

Jeff whistled. "Wow."

The skinny man came to the door again, and Donny went inside.

"Do you know that guy?" I asked Jeff.

He shook his head. "He's not too friendly, is he?"

"That's for sure. I wonder what they're doing?"

Jeff shrugged. "Donny said he was running an errand for somebody."

"Well, I hope it's not going to take much longer," I said. Twilight was beginning to fill the yard with shadows. I didn't want to miss the fireworks, and I didn't want Jeff's and my friends from school to miss seeing *us*.

"Here he comes," said Jeff.

Donny came out empty-handed and walked toward the car, a satisfied look on his face.

"All *right!*" he said happily, swinging into the front seat and drumming his hands on the steering wheel. "Let's go. I promised you guys a party!"

The Tomahawk jounced along through the gathering darkness, the headlights picking out first a deer, then a family of skunks. Finally, we were back on the main road, heading toward Oak Bluffs where the fireworks display and all the food stands were. Donny cruised slowly along the beachfront road, where hundreds of people had already claimed prime seats on the breakwall.

"Hey, there's Jason and Eric and the guys," I said, leaning into the front seat and pointing toward a group of kids from school. "Honk, Donny!"

Donny obliged, giving the Tomahawk's horn three quick taps. I slid across to the other side of the car and leaned out the window. Jason's jaw dropped when he saw Jeff and me waving from the windows of the Tomahawk. The other guys didn't even try to hide their envy. Eric gave me the "thumbs-up" sign, and I waved, trying to look cool and casual, as if I rode around with Donny Madison every day of the week.

Next we passed a group that included Jen Navarro, Donny's girlfriend. I saw her father frown as she waved excitedly and walked over to the car. Donny stopped, with the engine running, and Jen leaned in the driver's-side window to give him a kiss. Her long dark hair blew about her face, and I watched the way Donny sat back afterward, draping his arm across the open window, as if it was only natural that a beautiful girl like Jen should want to kiss him.

"So," he said lazily, with a teasing tone in his voice, "how's the family?"

Jen made a face. "I can't believe Daddy's making me spend the whole weekend with my cousins. I mean, they're okay, I guess." She looked deep into Donny's eyes and smiled. "But I'd rather be with you."

I couldn't help imagining what I'd do if a girl ever looked at me like that. I was pretty sure I'd never be able to be as cool as Donny, who reached up, gave her a little pretend punch to the chin, and said teasingly, "Yeah, well, Daddy knows best." There was a quick beep from behind, and Donny glanced in the rearview mirror. "Gotta go. We're holding up traffic here."

Jen, looking sad, mouthed the words, Call me, as we

pulled away. I couldn't see Donny's face, but if Jen had said that to me, I'd have been mouthing back, I will, I promise.

"Wow," said Jeff. I was thinking pretty much the same thing, but never would have said it out loud.

Donny looked at Jeff and laughed. "Don't get any big ideas, Manning," he said. "She's a little old for you."

Jeff looked really embarrassed. "I know, man. I didn't mean anything. I was just—"

Donny laughed again and said easily, "No sweat. Jen has that effect on guys."

I saw another group of kids from school and called out the window, "Hey, Mulvey!" It was great to watch Todd Mulvey's face, looking first puzzled, then impressed, when he saw Jeff and me in the Tomahawk.

I kept watching for kids I knew, waving casually to them from my place by the window, as Donny drove slowly down the avenue.

When the first flurry of fireworks went off, loud *oohs* and *aaahs* rose from the crowd. I waited to see if Donny was going to park someplace where everybody would be able to see us. To my surprise, he began heading away from town.

"Hey, Donny," I said. "Where are we going?"

"You'll see," he said mysteriously. After a minute or two, he pulled into a parking area near what everybody

called "the little bridge." It was a good spot to fish sometimes, but why the heck was Donny coming here now?

I was about to ask when he turned to flash me his
devil-may-care smile. "Trust me, Daggett," he said.

He turned off the engine, and in the sudden quiet the
sound of a firecracker exploded through the night. I saw a
glow followed by a faint trail of sparks falling through the
sky.

"We'll be able to see from here," Donny said. "And
now I've got a surprise for you guys."

He turned around to face me and said, "Reach under
the seat, will you? Right in the middle."

I felt blindly under the seat until my fingers touched a
paper bag, which I pulled out and held up. I could feel
that it was a bottle, full of something. "This?" I asked.

"Yeah. Keep looking. There's more."

I found three more paper bags, all about the same size
and shape and weight, and handed them forward to Donny.

Donny pulled the bottles out of the bags, one by one,
saying, "Top-shelf brands, every one. Nothing but the best
for my friends. What'll it be, Manning? Vodka? Daggett,
maybe you'd prefer a fine imported rum." He opened one
of the bottles, held it to his mouth, and took a swig.
"Aaaah."

He swallowed, turned to look first at Jeff, then at me,

and burst out laughing. "Oh, man!" he said when he'd gotten hold of himself. "You should see your faces! Come on, guys, lighten up! It's summer vacation. Have a little fun."

Jeff looked stricken, his face a mixture of disbelief and dismay. I was sure mine looked the same. Donny had said we were going to "party." I didn't know what I had expected, exactly, but it wasn't this.

"What's the matter?" Donny teased. "Never caught a buzz before?" He laughed and drank again from the bottle, then handed it to Jeff. "Go ahead; try it."

I watched as Jeff took the bottle, staring at it as if it were a lit firecracker. At that moment, a string of real fireworks exploded, and I thought Jeff was going to jump out of his skin.

My head was spinning with every warning about alcohol I'd ever heard at school, from Mom and Pop, and even from Barry, who had to deal with the results of drunk-driving accidents in his rental cars. I sank as far into the seat as I could, grateful now that I was sitting in the back. I knew it was chicken of me, but I was glad Jeff was going to have to be the one to speak up first. I waited for him to say, "No, thanks, man."

But Jeff didn't say no. He lifted the bottle and took a small sip. "Hoo!" he cried, shuddering.

"Have some more," Donny urged. "It grows on you."

I watched, unable to believe my eyes, as Jeff took another quick slug.

And then, smiling shakily, Jeff turned around and held out the bottle to me.

Ten

JEFF AND I STARED at each other across the seat, the bottle raised between us. Donny, seemingly unaware of the incredulous, murderous looks I was sending Jeff, said, "Go for it, Ben."

I knew what I was supposed to do. *Just say no.* But I wondered if Mr. Nixon, the drug and alcohol counselor at school, had ever sat in a car with his best friend and a cooler, older kid watching him, waiting to see what he was going to do. I felt Donny's eyes challenging me in the rearview mirror, and decided to pull a really gutless move.

I raised the bottle to my mouth. Keeping my lips pressed tightly together, I took the tiniest sip I possibly could. I made my Adam's apple wiggle up and down, pretending to swallow more. Just that little taste was gross enough to make me shiver. But I tilted the bottle again and repeated my little performance.

"Whew!" I said, giving what I hoped was a convincing smile. "Not bad." I handed the bottle back to the front seat, and Donny took it.

"Hey, Daggett," he said, "reach under that seat again, would you? There's a couple of cartons of cigarettes under there somewhere."

Relieved to have my turn over, I began feeling around beneath the sagging foam cushion. It was a good thing I was already leaning down, doubled over, because my mind made a sudden connection that hit me like a punch in the stomach: *cigarettes, liquor, expensive fishing equipment*—those were the things that had been stolen the night before from the cabin cruiser at Menemsha harbor!

I sat bolt upright, banging my head against the seat in front of me. "Donny!" I said, the words bursting from my mouth before I had time to think. "Where did you get this stuff?"

Donny paused midswig, then raised the bottle and swallowed more. Slowly, he lowered his arm and turned to face me.

The fireworks display began in earnest then, with an ear-splitting volley of deep booms. The whole sky lit up, white, red, blue, then white again. Donny's face flashed eerily before my eyes, illuminated one moment by color and light, cast into shadow the next. His features appeared friendly and familiar one moment, strange and sinister the next. I stared, mesmerized, all kinds of mixed-up emotions exploding inside me, as the show went on.

When there was a pause in the action, Donny turned away. In the darkness and quiet that followed, he said, "Ask me no questions, Daggett, and I'll tell you no lies."

Silence followed this remark, dragging on unbearably, as we all sat frozen in place.

Then Donny swore under his breath and said, "You guys are about as much fun as a fart in a phone booth." He took several more long drinks, then muttered, "Okay, Sherlock. Congratulations. I'm the one who hit that guy's boat."

Jeff glanced at me out of the corner of his eye, but neither of us spoke. I felt kind of stunned.

Slouching angrily in the front seat, Donny opened a pack of cigarettes and lit up. The fireworks started again, and he watched, concentrating on blowing smoke rings, ignoring Jeff and me completely. Even with the windows open, I began feeling a little sick.

At last the fireworks built to the grand finale and came to an end. In the quiet that followed, Donny let out a sarcastic laugh. "For crying out loud, you guys are acting like I mugged a nun or something. It's not that big a deal."

After taking another drink, he added, "Think about it,

Ben. The guy who owns that cabin cruiser is loaded, right? What's a couple of rods and reels to him? He can just go out and buy new ones, no sweat. Whereas I sell them and I make more money than I've ever had in my life."

Jeff caught my eye again and spoke up. "Yeah. It's not like you took them off one of us."

I thought, *There it is again: us and them.*

"My point exactly," Donny said, smiling and slapping Jeff approvingly on the arm. "I mean, you guys know what's going on, don't you?" he asked. "These people from outside, they just keep coming, buying up houses and land, making all the prices go up. So you know what? Pretty soon, people like us—people who were born here—we're not going to be able to afford to live on our own freakin' island. They're taking over, man."

"It stinks," Jeff said boldly.

"You're darn right it stinks," Donny said emphatically, taking another slug from the bottle. His voice was starting to sound funny, kind of thick and slow. "Sometimes when those fat cats bring their cars into the garage, I feel like—" He paused, as though he'd lost his train of thought for a minute.

"Daggett," he said finally, "how do you feel when your mother comes home from Town Hall and tells you how she put up with grief from tourists all day?" He mimicked a bossy female day-tripper: "I want my beach pass *now!*"

"Lousy," I admitted, glad that Donny was directing his anger at *them* rather than at Jeff and me. To keep his focus there, I added, "And you should have heard the guy Chick and I had on the boat today."

Jeff broke in eagerly. "Oh, yeah, you were going to tell me about that. What happened?"

Briefly, I told about the morning with Brad and Nicki. "I really felt like decking that guy!" I said, and the feeling I'd had that morning came back as strong as before.

"Exactly," said Donny, lighting up another cigarette, then taking another drink. "But you didn't, did you? You were nice and polite and you ended up getting stiffed."

"Chick didn't want Brad's money," I explained.

"Then Chick's an idiot," Donny said darkly. "He should have gotten every penny out of those jerks he could."

I tried to remember what else Chick had told me about not wanting Brad's money, but I couldn't. What Donny was saying seemed to make more sense, anyway. Not that I thought Chick was an idiot, but why not make Brad pay for being such a pain?

"Everybody flaps their mouths about how terrible things are getting," Donny said, "but nobody does anything. Well, *I'm* doing something." His words sounded kind of mushy, as if he had his mouth full of mashed pota-toes or something. "And you know what? It feels great. The guy who owns that boat I robbed is rolling in dough. I say, share the wealth. We share the island with him, right? He owes us. And I for one don't mind getting some of my own back."

Jeff said, "Right on, Donny."

"So I can trust you two to keep your mouths shut, right?"

"Right," said Jeff.

"Right, Daggett?" Donny repeated, his eyes in the rear-view mirror locked on mine.

"Right," I muttered, feeling really weird and confused. One part of my mind kept repeating things my parents had taught me my whole life, all of which added up to: what Donny had done was wrong. Period. End of story.

But, at the same time, something about what Donny was saying felt true. Was it really such a big deal, after all, to steal from a rich guy who could go right out and buy a new rod and reel any time he felt like it?

And even if Donny was wrong, what was I supposed to do about it? Was I supposed to tell on somebody I'd known all my life? For stealing something from a stranger who probably wouldn't even thank me?

As I was wondering about this, Donny straightened up in the seat, thrust the bottle at Jeff, and fired up the Tomahawk's engine. "I'd better get you kiddies home before your mommies freak, huh?" he asked, flashing his mocking grin.

With a squeal of tires, we pulled onto the highway. The bottle fell from Jeff's hands, and the potent, sweet-sour smell of alcohol filled the car. Jeff hurriedly fumbled for the cap and screwed it on, then passed all the bottles over to me. "Stick 'em back under the seat," he said.

I stuffed the bottles as far out of sight as I could. In my mind I heard Mom saying, *Ben, if you ever get into a situation where you're in a car and the driver has been drinking, just get out. Wherever you are, get out. Call me, and I'll come get you, you understand?*

Sure, I understood. It had all sounded simple when Mom and I talked about it, but now that I was in the actual situation, it wasn't as easy as she had made it sound. For one thing, I didn't know Donny was going to be drinking, and, for another, I didn't have time to get out of the car.

What was I supposed to do now, say, "Hey, Donny, stop and let me out. I feel like walking"? Did *Mom* understand how hard *that* would be?

"What's the matter, Daggett?" Donny would say. "Scared? You think I'm going to do something stupid like crack up the Tomahawk? No way, man. Don't worry about it."

I looked at the speedometer and saw that Donny was going close to sixty miles an hour. The highest speed allowed anywhere on the island was forty; the limit in most places was around thirty, sometimes even lower. Donny was asking for trouble by going sixty. If we didn't get into an accident first, we'd get pulled over for speeding, especially since it was the biggest weekend of the summer. And there we'd be, two underage kids with a driver who'd been drinking, in a car that reeked of stolen booze. Great.

Carefully, trying to sound cool, I said, "Hey, Donny, slow down, man. The cops'll be out tonight for sure. You don't want to get busted, do you?"

To my relief, Donny said, "Good thinking, Daggett. Trouble with the Tomahawk is, she wants to *go*. I really gotta watch this baby."

I kept an eye on the speedometer as it dropped to fifty, then forty, then thirty-five. *Keep it there, Donny,* I urged silently. *Let's just get home without anything happening.*

We did get home eventually, but not before I'd nearly had about seven heart attacks. Donny wasn't too good at handling the curves, and a couple of times when he was talking, he didn't even notice that he was driving on the wrong side of the road. Twice I couldn't help shouting, "Watch out!" and once Jeff reached over, grabbed the wheel, and steered us out of the path of an oncoming car.

At least Donny laughed about it instead of getting mad.

I was grateful for the lack of other cars on the road once we got up-island, and relieved when Donny pulled over on the stretch of road where we'd left our bikes.

"Thanks, man," Jeff said, getting out. "That was great."

"Yeah, thanks, Donny," I said, practically leaping out of the car.

"No problem," Donny replied. He smiled his lazy smile, seeming to have recovered his good mood. "What can I say? I got lucky, I shared the wealth. That's what friends are for, right?"

"Right!" Jeff agreed.

I was too nervous and jumpy to smile back. I just wanted Donny to leave.

"Adios, amigos," he said, and pulled away.

"Wow," said Jeff, turning to me with an excited grin on his face. "Can you believe it?"

"What?" I asked. "That we got home alive?"

"Well, yeah," Jeff said with a sheepish smile. "But I wasn't too worried about that. Donny wouldn't crack up his car."

Of course he wouldn't crack it up on purpose, I wanted to say but didn't. Lately I seemed to be doing a lot of keeping my mouth shut.

"I can't believe what he did," Jeff went on. "And the way he, like, really trusts us."

"Yeah," I replied, without enthusiasm.

"What's the matter? You seem kind of bummed out."

"I don't know," I said. "When Donny explains it, it sounds okay, I guess. I see what he means, you know? But . . . "

"What?" Jeff urged.

Right at that minute, I was really missing Pop. I'd been able to talk to him about almost anything. But now things were happening that I'd never had to discuss when he was alive.

Jeff was looking at me, waiting. When I didn't answer, he said slowly, "Look, your mom and my parents would say what Donny did was really terrible. But, like Donny says, they just don't get it."

"Yeah, maybe," I said.

"At least Donny's doing something," Jeff went on.

I almost told Jeff he was starting to sound like a parrot, repeating everything Donny said, but I didn't.

"I was freaked when he brought out the booze," I said instead.

"Donny said we were going to party," Jeff answered nonchalantly. He laughed, and punched my arm. "What did you expect? Cake and ice cream?"

I looked at him, feeling like a dumb little kid again. I'd been sure Jeff had been as surprised and nervous about drinking as I was, but maybe I'd been wrong. "Come on, Manning," I said. "You were surprised, too. Weren't you?"

"Well, yeah, sort of," he admitted.

Curious, I asked, "Did you like the taste?"

I was hoping he would make a gagging sound and say, "Are you kidding? That stuff was awful!" and we could laugh about how gross it was, the way we once would have.

But instead Jeff said, "It grows on you."

Like Donny says, I thought. "Look, I gotta go," I said.

Riding the rest of the way home on my bike, I practiced different conversations with Mom, who I knew would be waiting up for me. Part of me wanted to walk into the house and tell her everything, but another part of me wasn't sure.

Most grown-ups, Mom included, would think I ought to tell someone "in authority" about what Donny did.

But sometimes even grown-ups said it was bad to "tattle." I could still hear my third-grade teacher, Mrs. Wolnick, saying, "Nobody likes a tattletale, Ben. I'll take care of Charles. You take care of Ben."

My cheeks burned just remembering it. Charles had been shooting big, gross, germy spitballs into the fish tank, and *I* was the one who got yelled at.

The more I thought about it, the more confusing the whole thing became. For one thing, Jeff was my best friend, and he didn't seem to think what Donny had done was so bad.

For another, if I told on Donny, wouldn't he go to jail? How would that make me feel? How would I like being called a squeal, a rat, a snitch, a narc, a fink?

If telling was the right thing to do, why were the words for it so ugly?

Nobody likes a tattletale.

When Mom asked, I said the fireworks were great and went to bed.

Eleven

THE NEXT MORNING, Chick and I headed out of
the harbor with our charter for the day: a man named
Thad, who was pretty old, and his son, Jay, who looked
around Chick's age. As Chick steered the boat out beyond
the rocks at Devil's Bridge and around the clay cliffs of
Aquinnah, his face seemed even ruddier and more weath-
ered than usual. Pop's face had had that same warm, out-
doors look. Chick's hands on the wheel were brown and
tough, too, and strong, like Pop's. Thad and Jay had pale
white faces and hands, and their skin was smooth and soft
looking.

It was a chilly morning for early July, and Chick and
I both wore hooded sweatshirts, lobstermen's rubber
overalls and parkas, and rubber boots to protect us from

the wind off the water and the sea spray. By afternoon we'd probably strip down to jeans and T-shirts, if the day remained sunny.

Thad and Jay could have just stepped out of one of the expensive shops down in Edgartown. They had on brand-new skid-proof boat shoes, neatly ironed khaki pants, and sweaters with anchors and other nautical designs woven into them.

Chick and I; Thad and Jay. Us and them, I thought.

They were huddled miserably in the stern, trying to avoid the spray that showered into the boat every time Chick hit a wave. And there were plenty of waves, big ones, too, coming in from the northeast. Against the incoming tide, the wind caused a wicked chop.

In my head I could hear Donny laughing at Thad and Jay in their fancy clothes, saying, *Serves 'em right.* And part of me agreed. I mean, you just don't go out on the ocean, even in July, without being prepared for weather. Everyone around here knew that.

Still, I couldn't help feeling sorry for the two shivering men. Reaching into the storage area in the bow, I took out two spare orange parkas and handed them to Thad and Jay. "It won't be nearly as rough once we get around these cliffs!" I shouted over the noise of the engine. "Where we're going to fish, off Squibnocket beach, it should be pretty calm."

They put on the jackets eagerly, Jay smiling with relief and Thad giving me the "thumbs-up" sign. Chick gave me a wink.

When we got around what everyone called the head, the big point of land formed by the clay cliffs of Aquinnah, the seas settled into a light, even chop, and Thad and Jay began to look a lot happier. I began handing out rods and baiting them up, while Chick positioned the boat off Squibnocket point.

We planned to drift the shoreline for stripers. That meant we'd be continually watching out for rocks and starting the engine from time to time to keep us the right distance away from them.

Thad was using a sinking lure, trying to coax the fish up, and I was relieved to see that he was a decent caster. Jay was pretty clueless, so I showed him how to cast a chunk of bait with a smooth, even motion, let it sink, raise it up a bit off the bottom, and wait for the strike.

I was untangling a big snarl from Jay's line when Thad shouted excitedly, "I got one!"

After that, the day went quickly. Jay soon got the hang of casting, and we all relaxed. The only trouble was as soon as my mind wasn't occupied with working, I began to think about Donny.

Here it was, summer vacation, which was usually the best time of the whole year. Working with Chick and

93

making money was cool, and when I wasn't doing that, I was supposed to be messing around with my friends, carefree and happy. Instead, I felt weighted down by what I knew about Donny, almost as though I had an anchor tied around my neck.

I tried to concentrate on work, though, and I must have done all right because when we pulled into Menemsha at the end of the day, Thad and Jay thanked Chick and me over and over, and told everybody on the docks what a great time they'd had. They each gave me a ten-dollar tip, which just went to show that Donny wasn't right about *all* tourists. Why was it, I wondered, that the bad ones seemed to stick in everyone's minds, including mine, so much more than the ones who were nice?

Chick and I were cleaning up the boat when Pete came over to talk. As usual, he wore his battered hat, the word *Harbormaster* so faded you couldn't tell what it said unless you already knew. After hearing our report on the day's fishing, he said, "Well, the police were around today, asking questions. Apparently, the kid who was driving that car—Cameron Maddox—is still missing."

"It's been what—almost three days now?" Chick asked.

I thought back to Friday morning, when I'd discovered the car. "Yes," I answered.

"His parents were here, too," Pete said. "They've had posters made up and are hanging them all over the island."

He gestured toward one of the tar-soaked poles that held up the dock, and I saw a photocopy of a young man's face, with the words HAVE YOU SEEN OUR SON? across the top in bold black letters.

Curious, I leaned closer to read the small print below the picture: *Cameron Maddox, age 16, 5 feet, 10 inches, with green eyes, sandy blond hair. Missing since Thursday evening, July 2. Last seen in West Basin/Lobsterville Beach area, driving a red Porsche with Connecticut license plates. Anyone with any information, please call Mr. and Mrs. Maddox, c/o The Rosehip Inn, Edgartown.*

This was followed by a phone number and the word REWARD in the same big, black lettering.

I peered more closely at the photo of Cameron Maddox. It was your basic school picture, the kind everyone got taken every year. Maddox was smiling into the camera, as if he didn't have a care in the world.

Now he was missing. It was kind of creepy.

"The police were asking Marshall and all the young kids if they'd heard anything about this Maddox kid dealing dope," Pete said. "The parents are fit to be tied, saying the police are trying to ruin their son's reputation instead of finding out what happened to him. It got pretty ugly, I can tell you."

"Why would they say a thing like that?" Chick asked.

"Beats me," Pete said.

"Sounds as though they don't want to face facts about their kid," Chick mused. "That's got to be a tough one, having your son missing and finding out he might have been breaking the law."

I checked out Cameron Maddox's smiling face in the photo again. "He doesn't look like a drug dealer," I said.

"You never can tell," Chick answered.

Which was true. Donny didn't look like the kind of guy who'd rob a boat, either.

We crossed the channel to tie up at West Basin harbor, and I was happy to see Jeff there, waiting for us to come in. We all shot the breeze for a while. Jeff was excited because he had finished putting his plane together, and wanted to fly it.

After Chick drove off in his pickup, I was surprised to see Donny back out of a space in the parking lot and head over to us.

"Just the two gentlemen I was looking for," Donny said, pulling up alongside Jeff and me. "Hop in. I've got a proposition for you." He grinned enticingly. "This is your lucky day."

Twelve

I HESITATED, remembering the night before and how eager I'd been to get *out* of the Tomahawk. But Donny was acting as though nothing unusual had happened, and Jeff reached right down to lock his bike to mine, then jumped in the front seat. Reluctantly, I took what was starting to feel like my place in the back. Donny pulled into an empty parking space in the lot, and we sat facing the water. Cameron Maddox's face stared at us from a poster stapled to one of the town signs.

Donny shut off the engine, put his arm over the seat, and turned so he could look right at me. "So, how was the fishing today, Daggett?" he asked.

"Pretty good," I answered carefully. I was wondering what was up. I'd figured that after last night, he wouldn't want to hang out with Jeff and me again. And I'd thought that was fine with me. But now, face to face with Donny's magnetic personality and his contagious grin, it was hard to stay mad.

"How much money did you make?" he asked.

"Chick pays me thirty dollars a day, and today I got twenty in tips," I said proudly.

"That's pretty good," Donny said approvingly. "So, you got up at six A.M. and just got through, right?"

"Yeah," I said. "Why?"

Donny didn't answer, but instead asked Jeff, "Did you work today?"

Jeff made a face. "I spent half the day cleaning screens and washing windows for my mom."

"Did you get paid?"

"Twenty dollars."

Donny smiled. "How would you guys like to make almost that much for five minutes' work? Actually, it's not even work. For five minutes of your valuable time?"

"Get outta here," I said.

"No way," Jeff said at the same time.

"I'm serious," Donny answered. "I'm in on a really good business deal, and I'm giving you guys first dibs on a piece of the action."

"What do we have to do?" I asked cautiously.

"Just listen, for now. I had this great idea. It's so simple,

I can't believe nobody's thought of it before. Okay, you ready? You know how there's basically no stores or anything up at this end of the island?"

"How about *anywhere* on the island," Jeff said, moaning. "No malls, not even a McDonald's! I mean, there are McDonald's in *Russia*, for crying out loud, probably even in *Siberia*."

It was one of Jeff's constant complaints. Personally, I couldn't have cared less. I wasn't crazy about McDonald's food, and I'd rather be fishing any day than hanging out at a mall. I thought it was cool that the Vineyard was different from other places.

"Yeah, well, I'm setting up a little supply service for people who don't want to drive all the way down-island every time they need something," Donny said. "See, I'll get the orders together and make all the arrangements. All you guys have to do is make the deliveries on your bikes. I'll pay you fifteen dollars for every delivery. You'll make about ten deliveries a week each. That's a hundred and fifty bucks. What do you say?"

I looked at Jeff, shrugged, and smiled. It sounded easy enough. Too easy. "What's the catch?" I asked.

Donny gave me a quick grin. "No catch," he said. "People are lazy. They're willing to pay big bucks for convenience. You'll be mostly delivering to tourists. They've got money to burn."

I nodded. The ridiculous prices visitors were willing to pay for the silliest things was a constant source of amusement to islanders.

Then Donny's face grew serious. "The only thing is, you can't tell anybody about it. Somebody could steal my idea, cut into my profits, you know?"

That made sense. But I still didn't like the sound of it. "You really mean we can't tell *anybody*?" I asked.

"Nobody," Donny said sharply. "Not even your mother, Daggett," he added, then smiled. "Not that I think your mother's going to steal my idea. It's just that the fewer people who know, the better."

Jeff nodded eagerly, but I waited to hear more.

"So are you in, or should I ask somebody else? I've got to know now."

"Hold it a second," I said. I felt as if there were questions I should ask, but I couldn't think of what they were. I looked at Jeff, hoping he'd say something, but I could tell right away that he wanted to go for it. He was already figuring our profits in his head.

"Daggett, three hundred bucks a week between us! And that's not even counting money from our other jobs. We'll have that boat and motor by August!"

One problem immediately popped into my mind at that: how would I explain to Mom that I was going in on a boat and motor with Jeff, if I couldn't tell her where I'd gotten the money? I pushed it from my mind. I could worry about that later, when—and if—I had the money.

Then I had another thought. "What if I make a delivery to somebody who knows Mom? She'll hear about it. She always does."

"Not to worry, Daggett," said Donny. "Like I said, most of our customers will be people from off-island. I'll tell my local customers to keep their mouths shut about it."

It seemed odd: most businesses, like Barry's, advertised their services. Donny must have sensed my doubts, because he said, "Okay, another reason for the secrecy is that I'm not real sure this is strictly legal."

Uh-oh, I thought. *Here we go.* No wonder it sounded too good to be true.

"It drives a lot of people who are renting houses crazy that they have to drive all the way to Chilmark to pick up their mail, you know? So some of the stuff we deliver might be letters or packages, to save people a trip to the post office. And I'm not sure if that's against some bogus federal regulation, like horning in on the U.S. mail or something. So I'm just playing it safe, you see what I mean?"

"Yeah," I said. "I guess." Delivering a few letters didn't sound like a crime to me. I couldn't imagine why the U.S. post office would care. Donny probably *was* just playing it safe. But something was still bugging me.

Suddenly it came to me. "What do you need us for? Why don't you make the deliveries yourself? You've got a car."

"Believe me, I would if I could, Daggett," answered Donny. "But this business is already so big, I'm going to be busy just taking and filling the orders. Especially since I'm still working at the garage. I'm thinking, if we do this right, we all might be able to quit our other jobs soon and let the good times roll, you know?"

I nodded slowly, thinking it over. Not that I wanted to quit working for Chick. But the idea of making a hundred and fifty dollars more each week was growing in my mind, making it hard to think of anything else.

Donny looked at me and said, "Listen, Ben. I know you were kind of freaked when you figured out I stole that stuff. I know it's not your style. That's cool. But this is different. It's a way to make some good money without robbing anybody's boat. It's a *good* thing, Daggett."

I was surprised that Donny had even noticed I was upset the night before and more surprised that he actually seemed to care. It was almost as if he was apologizing, trying to make it up to me. He wanted to earn some honest money, and that *was* a good thing.

Then he said something that really got me. In a low voice, sounding almost humble, he murmured, "I've got to have some cash if I want to keep a girl like Jen happy."

Donny, Mr. Cool, was worried about losing his girl-friend? I remembered Jen's face when she kissed Donny. It had looked to me as though she really liked him.

"Aw, I don't think Jen's snobby like that," I said.

"Maybe not," said Donny. "But her family's got money. She's used to nice stuff. You didn't see her when that Cameron Maddox guy pulled up in his expensive sports car and asked her to go for a ride. She wanted to; I could tell."

Donny looked so downcast that I found myself feeling sorry for him. It was amazing to discover that a big shot like Donny had such thoughts.

"So," he said, looking at me from under his eyebrows. "What do you say?"

Before I could answer, Jeff said, "When do we start?"

Donny didn't react but continued to look at me, wait-ing. Jeff was watching me, too, his eyes willing me to say yes.

I gazed from one to the other and made up my mind. "Yeah, when do we start?"

"*All right,* Daggett!" Donny pumped his fist, then lifted his eyebrows tantalizingly. "How about right now?"

"Why not?" Jeff said, turning to me with a huge smile.

"No reason, I guess," I said. "I've got nearly an hour and a half before Mom gets out of work. I might as well use the time to make a little cash." *Why not?*

"Excellent. But first I need to know I can trust you."

Jeff looked wounded, and I felt the same way. "You can trust us, man," Jeff said. "You didn't see us telling anybody about the other stuff, did you?"

"No, and that's how I know I can trust you," Donny said soothingly. "Otherwise, I'd never have let you in. This is just to make it official. You don't talk to anyone about this. If anybody asks where the extra money's coming from, what are you going to say?"

"I could say it's from tips," I said.

Donny nodded. "Good. How about you, Manning?"

"From doing lots of lawns and odd jobs."

"Okay. No matter what, you never mention me, right?"

"Right," Jeff and I agreed.

"Okay." Donny extended his hand to Jeff, who shook it, trying to look solemn, but I could see the excitement shining in his eyes.

Next, Donny reached his hand over the seat to me, and I took it. I felt a thrilling jolt of heat and power as Donny looked into my eyes and tightened his grip. "Partners," he said, and gave me a wink.

"Okay," he went on, "your first job is to deliver these two packages right here." He reached into the glove compartment and took out two identical-looking manila envelopes sealed with the little metal fasteners bent shut and taped over.

"What's in them?" I asked. "Mail?"

Donny nodded. He handed one envelope to me and one to Jeff, and gave each of us directions.

"The person there will give you an envelope with the money in it. Bring it to me, and I give you your share. Simple."

"No problem," Jeff said.

"Where will you be?" I asked.

"Just stop by my house when you're done."

"Okay," I said. Donny lived pretty close to both Jeff and me. His father was never around, and his mom worked, so the coast would be clear.

I placed the envelope in the clip on my rear bike rack. My directions were to head down State Road, turn left at the white picket fence right before Ida Hill's house, where she sold homemade chocolates, go right at the next two forks, and look for a house marked with a big red *K* at the entrance to the drive.

I didn't know whose house it was, and it was probably being rented, anyway. Lots of people we knew lived in little dumpy shacks or moved in with relatives for the summer so they could rent their own houses to tourists for a lot of money.

As I rode down State Road, I saw HAVE YOU SEEN OUR SON? posters on almost every telephone pole. The Maddoxes had really covered the territory. I thought about when Pop was missing and how worried Mom and I had been, then how frantic she was last year when I'd run away during the night. I hoped that kid would turn up soon and give his parents a break.

I found the house and knocked at the door. A woman peered through the screen at me, looking puzzled. Then her face brightened. "Do you have a package for me?" she asked.

I nodded, holding up the envelope. She disappeared for a couple of seconds and returned with a regular letter-sized envelope, which she handed me in exchange for mine.

"Thanks," she said. She closed the door and was gone.

I rode to Donny's house and found him sitting in a lawn chair in the yard, working out some figures on a notepad. He took the envelope, looked in, smiled, and handed me a five and a ten.

"No problems?" he asked.

"Nope."

"Told you. Easiest money you'll ever make." Donny used the envelope to tap out a little rhythm against his thigh. "So, this time of day is good for you, right?"

"Yeah," I said. "Between four and five-thirty."

Jeff rode up on his bike, sweating slightly from the ride, but smiling. He handed Donny his envelope and collected his money, reporting that everything had gone smoothly for him, too.

After agreeing to meet at the West Basin parking lot around four o'clock the next day, Jeff and I biked home. We decided that if there was time after we'd made our deliveries, we'd go to the beach and try out the new plane.

"See you," I called, turning off at my house. I could feel the grin on my face and the significant bulge of sixty-five dollars in my pocket.

It was going to be a great summer after all.

Thirteen

THE NEXT MORNING, Chick greeted me with the words, "Ben, I hope you got a good night's sleep. We have a tough day ahead."

I groaned. "What does that mean?"

"We've got four guys, all meat fishermen."

I must have looked puzzled, because he explained. "They're going to want to catch and keep as many fish as they possibly can, and not release *anything*. They'll want to fill up their coolers with fillets, so they can go home and show off all the fish they caught, and tell themselves it was worth the price of the charter 'cause they're feeding their families. The only problem is, no matter how many fish we catch, they'll think it should have been more."

"Oh, boy," I said. "So what do you want me to do?"

"The main thing is to get the fish in fast and be ready to catch another one. These guys aren't going to want to play the fish, or enjoy the fight."

"Okay," I said. "But it kind of takes the fun out of it, don't you think?"

"I know, but this is their day, so we'll try to do it their way. I'll need you to keep a chum line going, and to keep the hooks baited."

"Aye, aye, Captain," I said. "One good thing, I guess: it won't be boring."

Chick laughed. "Oh, no," he said. "I can promise you that."

We were right, it wasn't boring. But I didn't look forward to fishing like that again. It became a day-long competition among the guys as to who had the most fish. I understand a contest. I always entered the annual island-wide fishing derby with everyone trying to catch the biggest fish and win. Well, everyone except for me in last year's derby, when I caught what was probably the winning fish and let it go. Anyway, I loved fishing and took it really seriously. But it was supposed to be fun. These guys were just serious.

Chick and I turned to each other after they left and smiled tiredly.

"All I can say is, I hope they actually eat all those fish I cleaned," I said. "And did you notice? No tip."

"I should have warned you not to expect one," Chick answered. "Not from those guys. But, listen, have you given any thought to working some more? I've got tomorrow off, but I'm booked for three days after that."

"Sure." I pretended it was no big deal, but I was really happy that Chick wanted me back.

"Good," Chick said, grinning and putting his arm around my shoulders. "You've been doing a great job, Ben. Your dad would be proud."

I never knew when it would happen, and it always took me by surprise. For some reason, at the mention of Pop, my eyes got all blurry with a sudden rush of tears. I didn't bother to turn away or pull the cap of my hat lower so Chick wouldn't see me cry. Chick understood how grief can sneak up and pull the rug out from under a person. His wife had had cancer and died about a month after Pop did.

"Yep," Chick went on, "we ran into some tricky situations the past few days. Jack would have liked the way you handled yourself."

Ordinarily Chick's praise would have made me feel great, but my insides felt uneasy. I'd been in a couple of tricky situations during the past few days that Chick didn't know about, and I was pretty sure Pop wouldn't have been proud at all of how I'd handled them. It was something I'd been trying hard not to think about. I reached up and roughly wiped the tears away, trying to brush away my disturbing thoughts, as well.

"Thanks, Chick," I managed to mumble.

"So you want to sign up for three more days?" he asked.

"Definitely," I said.

"Good. Same time Wednesday, then. Have a good day off, partner."

At that moment, Donny drove into the lot, music blasting as usual from the open windows of the Tomahawk. *My other partner,* I thought, feeling like a regular business tycoon.

I said good-bye to Chick and started walking toward the car. As I drew close enough to see Donny's face through the windshield, he shook his head slightly and waved me away, with a nod in Chick's direction.

I was confused for a minute, then figured out that Donny didn't want Chick to see me meeting him. It seemed to me Donny was going a little overboard with the secrecy thing, but I busied myself near my bike, fiddling with the shift knob, until Chick drove away.

Jeff showed up then, and Donny gave us two more envelopes to deliver. I was surprised that they looked pretty much like the ones from the day before. Were we going to deliver only mail? Anticipating the possibility of carrying something larger, such as groceries, I had dug my old basket out of the garage and put it on the handlebars of my bike. It looked as if I wasn't going to need it, at least not today.

My delivery was pretty close by, up a dirt road off the Moshup Trail. "This won't take long," I said to Jeff. "We'll have time to fly the plane when we're done."

"Mine will take a little longer, so I'll call you when I get home."

"Great. Let's go."

We raced each other up to where I had to turn off and Jeff kept going straight. Everything went pretty much as it had the day before, except this time it was a teenage guy who came to the door and took the envelope.

I pedaled as fast as I could back to Donny's to collect my money. As he handed me three fives, I caught a glimpse of a lot of other bills. "Tomorrow I'll meet you at the beach parking lot on the circle," he said.

"How come?" I asked.

"Just a precaution. Somebody might get wise to us if we keep meeting at the same place," Donny said casually.

I thought about how he hadn't wanted Chick to see us together that afternoon. "Okay," I said. Donny was making such a big deal about keeping our business secret. Maybe he was simply enjoying acting like a spy in a movie or something. I left, eager to meet Jeff and fly the plane.

When I got home, I called Mom at work. "Is it okay if I go to Philbin Beach with Jeff to fly his new plane?"

"What about dinner?"

"Could we eat a little later than usual? Like seven?"

"I don't see why not."

"Great. Thanks. Hey, guess what? I have tomorrow off and then Chick wants me to work for the next three days."

"That's wonderful, Ben."

"Yeah, I know," I said. "Jeff and I might even be able to get a boat before the end of the summer."

"That would take an awful lot of money." I could hear the doubt in her voice.

"If I keep getting big tips, who knows?" I said in a deliberate attempt to get Mom thinking I was making more than I really was working for Chick. I was a little surprised by how easy it was to lie to her, now that I'd gotten started.

Again that uneasy feeling squiggled through me, but I tried to ignore it. I wasn't doing anything wrong, really. As Donny said, I just had to keep quiet so nobody could steal our business.

Mom laughed. "Maybe I should quit here and work charters, too, Mr. Moneybags."

As soon as Mom and I hung up, Jeff called, and we

agreed to meet at the entrance to Philbin Beach. After hiding our bikes in a tangle of beach plums, we began walking up the beach past our secret cave in the clay cliffs toward a wide, open spot where we could launch the plane.

We neared the rocky point of Devil's Bridge, got the plane, the battery, and fuel ready, and were about to start to crank 'er up when something caught my eye.

"Look!" I said, pointing. A group of gulls was hovering excitedly over the water, their shrill, raucous cries making a racket that carried over the boom of the surf. Jeff and I had fished together enough times that I didn't have to say any more. When birds acted like that, it meant there was food around. Often, it meant that fish were feeding right under them, and they were hoping for scraps. Even though we didn't have rods with us, we had to take a look.

We both shielded our eyes from the sun, trying to catch a glimpse of a fin or tail beneath the screeching flock.

"There can't be fish there," I said after a minute. "The water's not deep enough."

"But there's something," said Jeff. "You see it?"

"Yeah," I said, squinting even harder. "Right near that big rock."

"Trash, probably," said Jeff.

"But how come the gulls are so excited?" I wondered.

"Cause they love garbage," Jeff answered.

"Yeah, but, wait a second . . . " I looked again. "What the—"

I couldn't have seen what I thought I'd seen. But there it was again. I began running toward the water.

fourteen

I DON'T KNOW how long I stood there staring, with the water sloshing over the tops of my sneakers. Overhead the gulls screamed, outraged at my intrusion. Jeff pulled up next to me, panting hard.

"Oh, God. No way. Oh, God," he said. "It's that kid, isn't it?"

I was sure Jeff was right. There were shreds of a green T-shirt and what looked like faded khaki shorts. Strands of light brown hair waved about like seaweed in the shallow water.

I continued to stare, frozen in horrified fascination, vaguely aware of Jeff breathing heavily beside me, and of my own blood pounding in my head. Then, in a voice edged with panic, Jeff whispered, "Daggett, let's get out of here."

Our eyes met. Jeff's were wide, and his face looked gray beneath the brown of his skin. Without another word, we turned away from the body in the water and bolted for our bikes.

We pedaled up the road, ditched our bikes in the town parking lot, and ran straight into the police station. Jeff's Uncle Cully was the sergeant at the desk. He smiled when he saw us and was about to say something, then looked closer at our faces and began to frown. "You boys look pretty shook up," he said. "What's the problem?"

I wanted to answer him, but something about the kindness and concern in his voice and the normal, safe, everyday surroundings of the room made the horror of what I'd seen seem even worse. I tried to talk, but instead began to cry—big, gulping sobs.

Any other time, I'd have been embarrassed, but I was too distraught to care. Besides, Jeff was crying, too. Cully, his face creased with worry, handed us tissues. Then he led us to an office in the back of the station and sat us down.

Jeff and I looked at each other. He said, "You tell, Ben. You saw it first."

"There's a body," I said. "A person. I mean, it was a person. Now it's—it's—" I remembered the waving strands of sandy brown hair, and the room began to spin.

Cully waited until I collected myself. "Where, Ben?"

"In the water. Almost up on the beach at Devil's Bridge."

"Did you move it or touch it?" Cully asked.

"No way," said Jeff, looking horrified.

"Good," said Cully. "Could you tell anything about the person? For instance, whether it was male or female?"

"It's that kid," I said. "The one who disappeared." But suddenly I wasn't sure. The body had been so weird and swollen, and the gulls had already been picking at it. I shuddered. It could have been anybody wearing shorts and a T-shirt, maybe even a girl with short brown hair. "I mean, we thought it was, anyway," I said uncertainly.

Jeff said, "Is it, Uncle Cully?"

"I don't know yet, Jeff," Cully answered. He stood up. "We'll have more questions for you boys, but right now I'm going to go talk to the chief. Will you be all right here for a minute?"

Jeff and I nodded.

"I'll call over to Town Hall and tell your mother you're here," Cully said to me as he left the room.

In what seemed like just a few seconds, Mom came flying into the police station from her office next door. "Ben!" she gasped, sitting down beside me and holding my face between her hands. "Are you all right?"

"Yeah," I said. I twisted my head and broke free. "I'm fine now. Really."

"Thank goodness." Turning to Jeff, she asked, "How about you?"

"I'm okay, Mrs. Daggett."

"You poor boys," Mom said. "What a terrible thing for you to see." Her voice drifted off as Cully and Chief Widdiss walked into the room.

The chief acknowledged us each in turn. "Hello, Kate. Ben, Jeff." His face, which usually reflected his cheerful good nature, was serious. "The sergeant is going to meet the state police down at the beach to recover the body. You say it's right in near shore at Devil's Bridge?"

Jeff and I nodded.

"The tide's coming in, Cully, and with this wind direction, you shouldn't have any trouble."

"Right, Chief."

"There's birds," I said, and my voice came out all croaky. I cleared my throat and added, "Gulls."

Cully grimaced, and I felt sorry for him, having to go down there. I was really glad the chief hadn't asked Jeff and me to go back. I thought about the search party that had found my father washed up on Cuttyhunk Island after the hurricane, and how awful it had been when Mom and I were told that Pop was truly dead.

I sneaked a look at Mom's face, and knew she was remembering the same thing. Somebody, somewhere was waiting for word about this person, and Mom and I knew what it was like to get that kind of news. I thought about Cameron Maddox's parents. Maybe they were rude, the way Pete and Barry had said they were, but if this turned out to be their son, I felt really, really sorry for them.

"Uncle Cully?" said Jeff. "Could you get my plane and stuff while you're down there? After we found the—the body, we just ran."

"Sure, Jeff," said Cully. "Don't worry, I'll get it."

Cully and Chief Widdiss excused themselves for a minute and left the room. Mom looked at me with a little line of worry between her eyebrows. "Are you sure you're going to be okay, Ben? Chief Widdiss would understand if you're not up to answering his questions right now."

"No, I'm okay, Mom. Honest," I said.

She leaned over to give me a hug, and when she pulled away, I saw tears in her eyes. I didn't know if they were for me, or Pop, or the poor dead person, or his family, and figured they were probably for us all. I hoped she'd go before I started crying again, and she did, giving my hand a little squeeze on the way out and saying, "I'll head home, then, and start dinner."

When she was gone, Jeff and I looked at each other. I

wondered if I looked as spooked as he did. "Ben," he whispered. "It's him, right? The Maddox kid?"

"It has to be, don't you think?"

Jeff whispered again, urgently, "Will they be able to tell what happened to him?"

I stared dumbly at him. Wasn't it obvious? "He drowned."

Jeff swallowed, looked nervously back over his shoulder, and said, "What if he didn't?"

"What do you mean?" I asked.

"What if Donny—" Jeff stopped, his eyes wide and scared looking.

Then I understood. Jeff was afraid that Donny had harmed more than Cameron Maddox's car.

"Will they be able to tell?" Jeff looked at me anxiously.

"Jeff!" I said. "Donny didn't—he wouldn't. You don't really think he *killed* the kid, do you?" The idea was preposterous.

"No." He hesitated. "I mean— No. But, Ben, he was mad at him and he *did* mess with the car, and if we tell, they're going to suspect him of messing with Maddox, too."

"But, wait. Maddox probably drowned, like I said. There's no reason for anybody to suspect Donny of murder."

"All I'm saying is, we've got to keep our mouths shut about the car. Act like we don't know anything."

We were quiet for a minute. The muffled voices of Cully and the chief grew louder as they approached.

"Just because Donny sank the car—" I began.

"Shhhhh!" Jeff just about jumped out of his seat. He looked at me, panic stricken. *"Don't tell!"*

Before I had a chance to answer, Chief Widdiss came back into the room. "Are you boys feeling better?"

Jeff and I both lied, "Yes, sir."

"Good. I'm sorry you had to be the ones to find the body," the chief went on. "It's not a pleasant experience, I know."

That's for sure, I thought.

"I need to ask you just a few questions, and then you can go on home. You were walking from the Philbin Beach parking lot up toward Devil's Bridge, is that right?"

"Yes," I said.

"And you came upon the body?"

"Well, we saw the birds first." I explained everything that had happened, ending with how we ran back to our bikes and came straight to the police station.

"Was anyone else at the beach? Did other people come over to see what you had found?"

"I didn't see anybody else." I looked at Jeff. "Did you?"

"I think there were some people farther up the beach sunbathing," Jeff said. "But nobody came over."

"And you didn't touch the body?"

"No."

"So, as far as you know, no one touched the body and no one else saw it except the two of you?"

We nodded.

"Good. Now, boys, I don't know if the body you found is Cameron Maddox's or not, but I'm betting it is. We'll know for sure pretty soon." The chief leaned across his desk and looked at us intently. "We've been hearing a lot of stories about this Maddox kid, about what he was doing here and what might have happened to him. We're trying to get to the bottom of it, and I wonder if you boys might have heard anything that could be helpful to us."

The silence stretched on and on. Afraid to look at Jeff, I kept my eyes straight ahead, which unfortunately meant I was gazing right into Chief Widdiss's face. His eyes moved back and forth from Jeff to me. The frown line in his forehead deepened as the silence grew.

Say something, Jeff, I urged. But Jeff didn't say a word. Finally, I couldn't stand it anymore.

"After he disappeared, I heard down at the dock that he might have been selling drugs," I said.

The chief's expression remained calm and interested. He didn't say anything.

After a while, Jeff spoke. "I heard his parents are pretty mad. They think somebody from here did something to him."

"Why would they think that?" the chief asked, almost as if he were talking to himself.

Jeff shrugged.

The chief turned to me. "Any ideas, Ben?"

"No," I said quickly, shaking my head. I could feel my face flaming bright red. Never before had I wanted so badly to disappear.

Chief Widdiss looked at Jeff then and said, "You didn't hear anything else from any of the older kids?"

"No," said Jeff, looking at his hands, which were squirming in his lap. His lie was just as obvious as my own.

There was another long silence. Chief Widdiss sighed and said, "If this body you found turns out to be Cameron Maddox's, and if it turns out that he did, in fact, meet with some sort of foul play, it will be a very serious matter. Do you realize that? We could be talking about a murder."

Jeff and I both nodded.

"If you know something that might help us in our investigation of such a serious matter, you must not withhold that information, do you understand?"

I swallowed hard and nodded again.

The chief sat back in his chair and folded his arms across his stomach. "I've known you two since you were knee-high," he said. "I know you're good boys. And sometimes good boys get themselves in a fix. They know something, or maybe just suspect something, about someone else, and they don't want to say anything about it. They want to protect a friend, or they don't want to 'rat' on him. Maybe they're even afraid of what will happen if they do."

The chief paused and looked from Jeff to me. "I want you to know that you don't need to be afraid. If you give me information, no one will know you were the ones to give it. You don't have to worry about falsely accusing someone, either. If something you heard turns out to be just a rumor, we'll find that out. You can't hurt anyone by telling what you know. But you can hurt yourselves, and maybe some innocent people, by keeping silent."

But keeping silent was what we did. I didn't know what I would have done if Jeff hadn't been there. I'd probably have told. I *wanted* to tell. It was scary to sit in the police station across from Chief Widdiss and *not* tell. Besides, I'd always liked the chief, and I wanted him to like me.

But Jeff and I were in this together. When Jeff didn't speak up, I felt as though I couldn't, either.

The chief must have seen in my face something of the struggle that was going on in my mind. He leaned forward again and said, "You can go now, boys. You know where I am if you decide you have something to tell me."

Jeff and I got up in a hurry. As we were walking out the door, the chief added quietly, "And I think you do."

Fifteen

JEFF AND I WALKED glumly out of the police station. I could feel the warmth of the asphalt parking lot through the soles of my sneakers, which were still wet from being in the ocean. The heat felt good. I'd been shivering in the chief's air-conditioned office, partly because it was cold but mostly because I was nervous and scared.

I kicked at a loose stone and said, "He knows we know something."

"Yeah, but he doesn't know *what* we know."

"I was kind of waiting for you to talk first," I ventured.

"I couldn't. I was totally freaking out!"

"Me, too! Jeff, we could get into real trouble for this! You can't lie to the police in a murder investigation!" I could hear something close to panic in my voice, but I didn't care if Jeff knew how scared I was.

"We didn't really lie."

"Oh, come off it, Jeff. Acting like we don't know anything when we do is the same as lying!"

"But, like you said, the kid probably drowned. So it's not a murder investigation. I don't even know why I said that about Donny doing something to Maddox. I was just—I don't know, everything was happening so fast."

I could feel myself beginning to settle down, now that we were out from under Chief Widdiss's probing gaze. Jeff, too, was losing his edgy look.

"Okay," he said, "so we *are* trying to protect somebody. But only because telling about the car could make them suspect that Donny did something worse."

"Right," I said. Out in the warm July sunshine, the idea that Donny had done anything to Cameron Maddox, let alone murder him, was just plain silly. "They'll do a whatchamacallit—an autopsy—and find out Maddox drowned, and it'll all be over."

"So there's no need to rat on Donny in the meantime," Jeff said.

"Right."

We didn't say anything for a while. Suddenly I felt very, very tired. "Well, I guess that's it for now. I'm going home," I said.

Mom and I were pretty quiet during dinner that night. Before she left work, word came in that Cameron Maddox's parents had definitely identified the body as their son's.

I swallowed and asked, "Do they know how he died?"

"The medical examiner is coming over from Bourne tomorrow morning. I suspect they'll find he drowned, but I suppose they'll be checking for evidence of drugs or alcohol, or anything that would explain why."

We spent the next couple of hours sitting together in the living room, staring at the television, but I don't think either one of us could have said what it was we watched. I went up to bed around eleven, but it was a long time before I fell asleep. My mind was zooming around like a remote-control airplane with a lunatic at the controls. I kept telling myself that what Jeff and I had done wasn't so bad.

But I couldn't hear Pop's voice agreeing with me.

Sixteen

I CONTINUED TO FEEL RESTLESS all the next morning, and I wished I had a charter with Chick to keep my mind occupied. Jeff was mowing lawns, so I just hung around the house. After lunch, Mom called to see how I was doing, and I asked her if Cameron Maddox's autopsy results were in.

"Yes," she said. "They found both alcohol and drugs in his system."

"So it was an accident," I said with relief. "He drowned."

"Well, he drowned, yes. But Chief Widdiss still hasn't ruled out the possibility that it wasn't entirely accidental."

"What's that supposed to mean?" I asked, trying to sound calm.

"I understand there's a wound on his head that looks suspicious."

"Couldn't he have hit it on a rock or something?"

"Apparently it doesn't look like that. Cameron Maddox was mixed up with selling drugs, Ben. When you get involved with that kind of thing, you put yourself in danger."

"So they think one of his customers *killed* him?"

"Ben, all I know is that his death is still under investigation."

When we hung up, I felt more agitated than ever. By a quarter to four, I was so happy to have something to do that I sped to the beach parking lot to meet Donny. He was waiting in the Tomahawk, and I could tell as soon as I slid into the seat next to him that something was wrong.

Donny, usually so cool and smooth, looked rattled. There was no lazy smile, no joking around. "What happened yesterday when you went to the cops?" he asked abruptly.

"Huh?" I said. "What do you mean?"

"What did you tell the cops?" he asked impatiently.

"Nothing," I said quickly. "Nothing about you, anyway. We found that kid—"

Donny interrupted me. "I know. I heard. But you didn't say anything about me? My name didn't even come up?"

"No," I said. "Honest."

He ran his hands through his hair in frustration. "Why are the cops coming around asking me questions, then?" he asked. But he seemed to be asking himself, not me, so I didn't say anything. "Manning didn't talk, either, right?"

"No way," I said. "We were together the whole time. They wanted to know about finding the body, and what we knew about Cameron Maddox. Nothing about you." There was a pause, and I said, "What are they asking you about, anyway? The car?"

"No," Donny said, looking distracted, not really paying attention to me. "I don't think they know about that."

"What, then?" Normally, I probably wouldn't have had the nerve to pump Donny so hard for information, but he wasn't acting normal, and I was curious. "The stuff you stole?"

Donny shook his head.

I lowered my voice, even though there was no one anywhere close. "Are they asking you about what happened to Cameron Maddox?"

"No," he answered, angrily this time. "Why would they do that?"

I shrugged.

Donny didn't push it. I could tell his mind was on something else. He spoke again, more to himself than to me. "Maybe I should call off deliveries this afternoon." He thought for a minute, then frowned and said, "Ray wouldn't like it, but—"

"Ray?" I said. "Who's Ray?"

Donny looked startled, as if he hadn't realized he'd been speaking out loud.

"Who's Ray?" I repeated. "And why would he care if I did my delivery or not?" The more I thought about this, the more puzzled I became. "I thought nobody knew about this except you, me, and Jeff."

From the window of the Tomahawk, we could see Jeff riding up the hill toward us. Donny turned to me and said urgently, "Forget Ray. He's nobody. And don't say anything to Manning."

Things were getting stranger by the minute. All of a sudden I was Donny's number one buddy, and Jeff was on the outs.

Jeff pulled up on his bike, calling, "Hi, guys. What's up?"

I could feel Donny still staring at me. Jeff looked back and forth from Donny's face to mine. We must have appeared pretty serious, because Jeff lifted an eyebrow at me questioningly. I shrugged and waited for Donny to speak first.

"You got deliveries for us today or what?" Jeff asked, looking baffled.

"Yeah," Donny said at last, in the tone of someone who had finally made up his mind. But he didn't seem thrilled about his decision. He reached into the glove compartment and took out two envelopes identical to the ones he'd given us on the two previous days. He handed one to me and one to Jeff.

"More mail? I thought we were going to be delivering different kinds of stuff," I said. "These packages all look the same."

Donny swore irritably. "Daggett," he said, "what'd I tell you before? Now, are you gonna do the job, or ask a bunch of stupid questions?"

Stung by this remark, which seemed unfair and un-partnerlike, I took the envelope from his hand and got out of the car. I was about to get on my bike and ride away without a backward glance, to let Donny know how ticked off I was, when I remembered I didn't know where I was going. So much for a dramatic exit.

I turned around to face him and waited for him to tell me the directions. Then I sat astride my bike while Jeff received his, and we rode off together.

"What's bugging him?" Jeff asked.

"I don't know," I said. I was nervous about Donny seeing us talking, afraid he'd think I was telling Jeff about Ray. At the same time I really wanted to tell Jeff. Something strange was going on. And there was definitely something Donny wasn't telling us about our little delivery business.

"Listen," I said. "Let's meet at my house after we make these deliveries, okay? And don't tell Donny."

Jeff gave me an odd look, but we were at the corner where we had to go separate ways. "I can't," he said. "I've got to go someplace with my parents."

"Then call me later, okay? And just act like nothing's up when you go back to Donny's."

I pedaled to the turnoff Donny had described, and headed down another sandy dirt lane. I was supposed to follow the red arrow at the fork, then turn at a hand-painted sign saying, PRIVATE WAY, NO BEACH ACCESS, and go to the third driveway after that.

I glanced behind me: no one in sight. There was no sign of anyone ahead, either. There was nothing but the smell of sun-baked dirt and the monotonous droning of insects in the undergrowth. I got off my bike and pushed it through the bushes that grew on both sides of the lane, sat down on a rock in a little clearing, and stared at the envelope in my hand.

Yes, something strange was going on. Donny was acting very weird. It was odd that all we'd been given to deliver were envelopes, all the same size, about the same weight, and, come to think of it, all with a little bulge at the bottom that indicated there was something more in them than just papers. From what Donny had said, I'd expected to be delivering sacks of groceries; or packets of mail containing people's letters, magazines, and newspapers; or maybe supplies from the drug store, shampoo and suntan lotion, Band-Aids, stuff like that.

But for three days in a row, I'd been carrying the same tightly sealed manila envelope. Donny hadn't told us the whole truth about our partnership, I was sure. And we'd been too dumb—too flattered by Donny's attention and too greedy for the money—to think it through.

But now my mind was flooded with questions. And I was filled with anger at Donny. He couldn't tell me what to do and what not to do, what I could say to Jeff and what I couldn't. He couldn't just blow me off, couldn't just say, "Forget Ray. He's nobody," and expect me, the dumb little kid, to reply, "Okay, Donny, whatever you say."

I was mad at myself, too, because I *had* been acting like a dumb little kid. But that didn't mean I had to keep it up. I meant to find the answers to my questions, and soon.

There was one little mystery, however, that I could solve right then and there. The one sitting in my lap.

My hands were trembling slightly as I slid my index finger under the tape and ran it the width of the envelope. I had to pinch the wings of the little metal fastener up underneath the tape to free the flap. Then all I had to do was look inside.

I could feel my heart starting to hammer in my chest. Part of me wanted to stick the tape back down and deliver the envelope as I'd done before. It was a crime to read other people's mail; what if that was all this was? How would I explain that I had opened it?

Looking at what I had done, I realized I *was* going to have to explain. There was no way I'd be able to get the tape to stick again and lie as smoothly as it had before. The damage was done. I might as well look.

I reached my hand inside the envelope, grasped the bulge at the bottom, and pulled out another envelope. Well, not an envelope, exactly, but a little bag. A little plastic bag just like the one Nicki had had with her on the boat.

One sniff and I knew exactly what it was.

The strange thing was, I wasn't really surprised. I guess I had known before, right from the beginning, that there was something suspect about our delivery service. I just hadn't wanted to think about it. I'd wanted to believe Donny, and to believe that it made perfect sense to deliver a package and be paid fifteen dollars.

"Easiest money you'll ever make," Donny had said, and I'd let him convince me because I wanted him to.

I felt like flinging the package into the bushes and leaving it there. I wanted to bike back home and pretend all of this hadn't happened, and never have to see Donny again. But I couldn't.

I had no idea how much the baggie in my hand was worth, but Donny was making enough of a profit to pay me fifteen dollars just to deliver it. And this Ray person who was going to be mad if Donny called off the deliveries, he had to be getting something out of it, too.

I imagined myself throwing the pot away and returning empty-handed. Donny would want his money. What would he do if he didn't get it?

"When you get involved with that kind of thing, you put yourself in danger," Mom had told me just that morning. I shivered, though I was drenched with sweat.

Cameron Maddox had been mixed up with selling drugs.

Cameron Maddox was dead.

Seventeen

I RESEALED THE ENVELOPE as neatly as I could, but anyone could tell that it had been opened. Since I was afraid to throw it away, I didn't see what else I could do except go through with the delivery.

And never make another one.

How was I going to explain that to Donny?

I sat in the clearing for a few more minutes, trying to fight the panic that kept welling inside me, trying to think. I decided to make the delivery, meet Donny afterward as if nothing unusual had happened, then talk to Jeff and tell him what I'd discovered. Together, we would decide what to do next.

I wheeled my bike furtively back onto the sandy lane, and began looking for the red arrow at the fork in the road. I hated the way I kept looking back over my shoulder, hated the fear and paranoia I felt from knowing what was in the envelope.

At last I came to the third driveway after the PRIVATE WAY sign, and knocked on the door of the house. But first I pulled down the brim of my baseball cap to cover my face.

An oldish guy came to the door, which kind of surprised me. I'd never really thought about it much, but I guess I figured it was mostly kids who smoked pot. Behind the man I caught a glimpse of a woman in a long, floaty kind of dress. She went to get a small envelope, which she gave me as I handed the manila one to the guy. He turned it over and made a funny face. Before he could say anything about the rumpled tape job, I ran to my bike and fled.

I pedaled hard, looking over my shoulder again, this time to make sure the man wasn't behind me. When I got to Donny's, the Tomahawk was parked in the yard, and he was in it, waiting.

I took a deep breath and pulled up warily beside the driver's side door. Something didn't feel right. Then I realized the radio was quiet. So was Donny. He was smoking nervously, raking his hair back from his face and scowling.

I handed him the envelope.

"Anybody follow you?" he asked.

"Follow me?" I repeated, playing dumb. "Why would anyone follow me?"

He didn't answer, but asked insistently, "So, nothing out of the ordinary happened?" It was strange to see Donny like this, not even pretending to act cool.

"No," I lied. I even managed an offhand, "The usual. Piece of cake."

Donny reached into the envelope, did a quick count, and handed me a ten and a five.

I was debating whether I should ask him what he was so worried about. Maybe I would have if I didn't already have some idea of the answer. I decided instead to get out of there as quickly as I could. "See ya, then," I said, getting ready to ride away.

I was hoping Donny wouldn't call me back to set up a delivery for the following day. To my relief, he said, "Take the day off tomorrow, Daggett." He tried to grin, but it didn't quite come off. "Wouldn't want you to work too hard."

"Okay," I said, pretending to be disappointed. "You're the boss."

I said it, but I didn't believe it anymore. Donny was Jeff's and my boss, but I was pretty sure somebody else was his boss. Namely, Ray.

I rode home, my hands shaking and my mind spinning

like the light on top of Chief Widdiss's police cruiser. The chief was on my mind, no doubt, because I had *just finished making a drug delivery.* The full realization of what I was involved in hit me, and I began trembling all over.

Jeff had said he was going somewhere with his parents, but when I got home I called him, hoping he hadn't left yet. "Jeff?"

"Yeah, what's up? You sound funny."

"Did you make your delivery?"

"Yeah, why?"

"Did everything go okay?"

"Yeah. Donny kept asking me the same thing. What's going on?"

"Listen, Jeff—" I began, then broke off, suddenly worried about talking over the telephone. In the movies, the cops were always tapping the bad guys' phones and tape recording what they said. But I wasn't one of the bad guys! And neither was Jeff.

Not really.

Even though it surely looked that way.

"How long are you going to be out tonight?" I asked.

"I don't know. We're going to my aunt's birthday party. It could be pretty late."

"Oh, great." I moaned. Then, abandoning caution, I blurted out the news that we'd been delivering drugs for Donny. I couldn't stand being the only one to know; I needed Jeff to tell me we weren't in as big a mess as I thought.

But instead a long silence met my words. Then Jeff spoke, his voice sounding small and shaken. "No way, Ben. You're kidding, right?"

When I didn't say anything, he whispered, "What are we going to do?"

I swallowed hard. "I don't know," I said.

Jeff whispered again. "My mom's right here, so I can't talk. I'll call you when we get home, unless it's really late."

"Okay." It wasn't okay, of course. I was so wired, I couldn't imagine sitting around, waiting for Jeff to come home, and I had no idea what I should do. The clock said a quarter after five. Fifteen minutes until Mom got home.

I decided to ride back to Donny's house. Before I told anybody else, like Mom or Chief Widdiss, I figured I'd better talk to Donny. Maybe he didn't know what was in the envelopes. Maybe this guy Ray, or whoever was the real boss, hadn't clued Donny in, and that was why Donny hadn't told Jeff and me.

Yeah, I thought, *and maybe the stuff in the envelopes will turn out to be spices for making spaghetti sauce.*

Still, even though I didn't really think Donny was innocent, or at least as innocent as Jeff and I were, I wanted to talk to him. Maybe there was some explanation that would make everything all right again. Maybe he'd say something that would mean I wouldn't have to rat on a guy who'd once been my hero, which also meant ratting on my best friend and myself.

There I went with the maybes again.

Eighteen

WHEN I PULLED into Donny's driveway, the Tomahawk was gone. Donny wasn't there, but the guy Donny had taken the reels to, the skinny little guy with the long, greasy ponytail, was.

Ponytail was walking from Donny's front door to his car, looking furious. It was too late to escape. He'd already seen me.

"What are you doing here?" he asked suspiciously.

I wanted to say, "I have as much right to be here as you do," but he didn't seem like the kind of guy I wanted to provoke. "Looking for Donny," I said, trying to act cool, even though he gave me the creeps, big-time.

He looked closer at me. "Which one are you, Manning or Daggett?" he asked.

Surprised that he knew our names, I answered, "Daggett. Ben."

Apparently, Ponytail had no intention of telling me his name. Instead he walked right up to me, grabbed me by the chin, and jerked my face up close to his. He wasn't much taller than I was, and I got a better look than I cared to at his stubbly whiskers, bad complexion, and brownish stained teeth as he said, "You the one who got nosy this afternoon?"

"W-what are you talking about?" I said. With his hands roughly gripping my chin and his narrowed eyes boring into mine, I felt terrified and helpless. Nobody was home at Donny's. Ponytail and I were alone in the yard, and no one knew where I was.

"You didn't have a little look-see at your delivery today?" he said. "Didn't snoop in other people's private business? Maybe help yourself to a little product?"

"N-no," I managed to choke out.

He gave my chin a twist to the side and let go. "If you're lying, I'll find out; you can bet on it," he said. "In the meantime, remember this. And you can tell your pal Manning, too: you steal from me, and I promise you'll be sorry. And if you're thinking of running to the cops, forget it. You two are in this thing right up to your ears. If I go down or Donny goes down, you go with us. Got it?"

I nodded, too frightened to speak.

"Ever been to the juvie farm?"

"The what?" I asked.

"Juvenile reform school," he said slowly, emphasizing every word.

I shook my head.

"Well, take it from me, you don't want to go there." He spat onto the sandy driveway, then added, "If you see our friend Donny, tell him I'm looking for him."

He got into his car and drove away, but not before giving me a long, meaningful stare that kept me frozen in place until he was well out of sight.

I'd broken into a sweat in Ponytail's grasp and now, in the breeze, my body was covered with goosebumps. I rubbed my arms and then my face, trying to snap out of the terror that Ponytail had made me feel, and *think*.

Ponytail was Ray, I was pretty sure about that. Ray, who wouldn't have been happy if Donny called off the day's deliveries; Ray, who must have been informed that the manila envelope had been opened, and who suspected I'd taken some of the pot. Ray, who knew all about juvenile reform school.

Ray, Donny's boss. My partner in crime.

I swallowed a sob that threatened to escape from my throat. How in the world had I gotten myself into such a screwed-up mess?

Getting in was easy, stupid, I answered myself. *Getting out is going to be the hard part.*

I'd never felt so alone in my life. And Pop had never seemed so far away.

I had to figure this out on my own. I hadn't imagined the sense of menace Ray projected. If things started to fall apart, and it looked as if they had, what might Ray do?

The sight of Cameron Maddox's body washing back and forth in the shallow waters off Devil's Bridge filled my mind. I pushed the picture away, telling myself I was being ridiculous to make a connection between Ray and a kid from off-island who happened to come here and drown.

I had no idea where Donny was, and neither, apparently, did Ray. But I knew I wanted to find him before Ray did.

Nineteen

AFTER SITTING THROUGH an endless dinner with Mom and Barry, pretending everything was just fine and totally normal, I asked if I could go out for a while.

"Where, Ben?" Mom asked.

"Just up to Jeff's," I said.

"But I saw June today, and I'm sure she said they were having a surprise party for Anita tonight."

"Oh, yeah," I said, acting as if I'd just remembered, and angry with myself for forgetting that Mom knew everything. "Well, then," I went on, thinking hard, "I kind of feel like taking a few casts down at the beach. I heard the blues were in." Lies piled on top of lies as I talked.

"Hey!" said Barry enthusiastically. "I'd like to go along

with you, Ben. You were going to teach me to cast this summer, remember?"

"Oh, right," I said, thinking miserably, *This nightmare doesn't go away; it just gets worse and worse.* I didn't want to hurt Barry's feelings—and Mom's, too—by saying no, but I couldn't have Barry coming with me. "The thing is, I don't know where the fish are, exactly. How about if I scout around tonight, kind of check out the situation, and we can go catch 'em tomorrow night?"

It was a lame excuse, and it sounded like one. Barry quickly tried to hide the expression of hurt on his face, and Mom gave me a long, probing look. I felt like a total creep.

"All right," Mom said carefully. "You do that. But be home no later than nine-thirty. You're working tomorrow, right?"

"Yeah," I said hurriedly, wanting only to get out of there fast. "I'll be back by nine—and I'll check out those fish, Barry. We can go tomorrow, like I said, okay?"

I ran upstairs to my bedroom. I had an idea. I reached into one of Pop's old tackle boxes, where I kept his good watch and all my other special stuff, including my money, counted out ninety dollars, and put it in my pocket. Ninety dollars. Forty-five for me, and forty-five for Jeff. It was the money we'd gotten from Donny, and I planned to give it back.

Then I grabbed a rod for show and looked around for a flashlight. The only one I could find was a heavy-duty waterproof torch Pop and I used to use in the boat, so I took it and threw it into my bike basket. Calling goodbye to Mom and Barry, I hit the road.

I checked out Donny's house first, and his mother told me he hadn't come home for dinner. Not only that, but she said the police had been there looking for him, too. She looked pretty frazzled, and I felt sorry for her. I could tell she didn't know whether to be angry or worried or both. I promised that if I found him, I'd tell him to come home, and left.

I knew what I was doing was stupid. Donny could be anywhere, even way down-island. He could have left the island on the ferry or on somebody's boat, especially if he knew the police were looking for him. Still, I cruised around looking for the Tomahawk, checking the parking lots at the cliffs and at West Basin. Posters with Cameron Maddox's picture still fluttered from almost every telephone pole, and I tried not to look at them.

I was riding down from the cliffs along the Moshup Trail, heading to the Philbin Beach lot, when I spotted a gleam of silver in the middle of the dense scrubby trees, beach grass, and poison ivy that lined the road. I circled back, and there was the Tomahawk, pulled off the road and nearly invisible in the underbrush. If I'd been in a car or if

I'd looked the other way for just a second, I'd never have seen it.

I stopped for a minute to think. It stood to reason that Donny was somewhere close by. He might be at somebody's house, but I couldn't imagine whose. There were no homes on the beach side of the road, where Donny's car was. The ones on the other side of the road were pretty far away, and were in all likelihood rented for the summer to tourists. That left the beach.

Donny really must have wanted not to be found. There was no way he could have gotten out of the Tomahawk and down to the beach without getting all scratched up, with a good case of poison ivy, as well. I sure wasn't going to follow that route.

I raced down the road about a half mile to the Philbin lot, and chained my bike to the rack. I didn't really need the rod, so I hid it in the bushes, but I took the flashlight with me. The parking area was deep in shadow. I checked my watch. It was already 8:30! It would be dark soon, and Mom would be waiting for me. I ran up the wooden boardwalks that made a path through the dunes and out onto the beach.

My plan was to work my way back toward where Donny had left his car, then continue in the direction of the cliffs and Devil's Bridge, until I found him. I kept running, scanning the narrow beach for any sign of Donny.

There were a few couples sitting around a fire, and farther on I passed a woman stretched out on a blanket, doing some kind of weird exercises.

Tourist, I thought scornfully. Then I caught myself. Okay, so some tourists were strange and some, like Brad and Nicki, were real jerks. So what? Donny was an islander—what about him? Was he supposed to be my friend, no matter what, just because he was one of *us*? I knew better now.

As I walked, I planned what I was going to say if and when I did find Donny. I figured there was only one way out. I had to come clean, to tell Chief Widdiss everything. And I wanted to give Donny the chance to come with me. Not because he was an islander, certainly not because I was awed by his coolness, which I wasn't anymore. Maybe because I'd known him my whole life and had been grateful to him more than once. It was possible that Donny had gotten sucked into trouble the same way I had, little by little, and that he wanted to get out, too, and didn't know how to do it.

Anyway, dumb as it sounded, that was my plan.

The sun was close to the horizon, with that squashed look it gets right before it sets for good. I had a couple more minutes of daylight left, and there was still no sign of Donny. I kept moving, past Devil's Bridge and up around the headland of Aquinnah, where the beach was a thin rocky strip between the ocean and the steep clay cliffs.

The tide was high: I couldn't go any farther without going swimming, and unless Donny had come much earlier than I, he hadn't gone any farther, either. I stood panting, ready to scream with frustration. Had I reasoned wrong? Where else could Donny be?

It struck me all at once: the cave. As far as I knew, Donny was the only person who knew about it besides Jeff and me. If he wanted to hide, I couldn't think of a better place.

Twenty

EVEN IN THE GATHERING DARKNESS, I had no trouble making my way up the cliffs to the cave. The climb was as familiar to me as the crash and hiss of the waves and the taste of the salt on my lips. I turned sideways to slide in the narrow opening and said, "Donny, it's me."

My words echoed eerily back to me, followed by a deep silence. I felt the first stirrings of doubt. Could I have been wrong? What, after all, had made me so sure Donny would be here?

But then a low whisper came from the depths of the cave. "Daggett?"

To my surprise, my own voice sounded clear and strong. "Yeah, it's me. I thought you might be here."

I didn't turn on the flashlight, even though I couldn't see Donny in the back of the cave. I was remembering something Pop had told me about cornered animals. He said you didn't want to stare directly at them, or crowd them, or make any sudden moves. You had to let them get used to you, and let them know you meant them no harm. It occurred to me that Donny probably felt just like a cornered animal, especially if he knew that Ray and the cops were looking for him.

"What are you doing here?" he asked.

"Looking for you," I said. "What are you doing?"

He laughed, but it wasn't a happy sound. "Good question."

I had to get on with what I'd come for, quickly, and get home. "Listen, Donny."

"Yeah?"

"I opened the envelope today and saw the dope. And I ran into Ray, and he's looking for you. And so are the cops, I think." I was talking really fast, trying to get it all out at once. "And, anyway, I don't want to do deliveries anymore, and neither does Jeff."

I didn't actually know that for sure, but I thought it was a pretty good guess.

"So, here." I reached into my pocket and took out the money I'd brought. "That's ninety dollars. Forty-five for me and forty-five for Jeff. It's what you've paid us so far. We're out."

Donny laughed again, bitterly. "You think it's that easy, Daggett? Just give back the money and you're out?"

"Yeah," I said uncertainly. "Why not?"

Donny made a strangled sound somewhere between a cry and a moan. "Oh, man," he said.

Now that my eyes were becoming used to the darkness, I could see him put his head in his hands and shake it back and forth.

"This is all so *screwed up*!" His voice rose in anger or despair, I couldn't tell which. "It's just a matter of time, anyway."

"Until what?"

"Until I get busted. Until we all get busted. And maybe even charged with murder." Donny broke off with something that sounded like a sob.

This sure wasn't the tough-talking Donny who'd taken me to the fireworks and bragged about getting some of his own back. This was a kid who was just as scared as I was.

"Murder? You mean Cameron Maddox?"

"That stupid jerk! I wish he'd never come here."

"But you didn't . . . " I didn't really want to ask, didn't want to know.

"Kill him? No!"

"Then why would you get blamed for it?"

He didn't answer, but asked instead, "You said you met Ray?"

"Yeah. He was at your house."

"Well, Ray's the one who's in charge of our little business. I guess you already figured that out. Maddox came to the island with a couple pounds of dope to sell to Ray. Except after the deal was made, Ray discovered that the order was a few ounces short, and he totally flipped out. You don't want to be around Ray when he's mad, I can tell you. He's little, but he's mean. The next day, Maddox was missing."

"Then Jeff and I found him—"

"Dead."

"You think Ray—?"

"I don't know," Donny said with a groan. "The whole thing is so messed up. The cops know Maddox was into drugs. I'm pretty sure they know about us, or why do they keep coming around asking questions? How long before they put it all together?"

I didn't know what to say.

Donny went on. "And the other stuff I did just makes it look worse. Pushing the car in the water was kind of a joke that got out of hand. But if they know I did it, it'll be easy for them to think I killed him, too, right?"

"Maybe. But are you sure he was murdered and didn't just drown? I mean, do the cops know for sure?"

"From the questions they're asking, believe me, they suspect something. They even went to Jen's house. Can you believe it? She broke up with me. I figured her old man made her do it, but she said she didn't want to hang out with a druggie." Donny laughed bitterly.

I took out the flashlight and checked my watch. Nine-fifteen. Mom was already mad.

Not nearly as mad as she's going to be, I thought. But I had come to find Donny with my mind made up about what I was going to do, and I didn't see any reason not to go through with my plan. I turned on the flashlight and shone it on the back wall of the cave until I found the place where Pop's initials were carved, right near Jeff's and mine. Seeing the letters JUD, for Jack Ulysses Daggett, gave me courage.

"Donny, the reason I came to find you is because—" I faltered for a moment. "I'm going to the cops."

"You're *what*?"

"Look, Donny, I wanted to warn you first and give you the chance to go with me. I'm sure it'll be better that way, better than getting caught. I'm going to tell them everything I know and hope—" My voice broke as I thought about getting sent to juvenile reform school. I swallowed and went on. "Hope they won't be too tough on us."

"Ben, you *can't*," Donny said, desperation in his voice.

"See, you and Jeff won't get in too much trouble because you're minors. That's why Ray wanted me to hire you guys. But I'm over sixteen, man. I could go to *jail*."

I was still standing close to the cave's entrance, facing inward toward Donny. A voice came suddenly from behind me. "That's right, Donny."

Startled, I dropped the flashlight. With shaking hands, I fumbled for it in the dark, then tried to hold it steady as I pointed it in the direction of the voice.

The powerful beam illuminated the scowling face of Ray.

"And that's why nobody's going to the cops," he said. Then he swore and held a hand up to cover his eyes. "Turn that thing off!" he ordered.

But I didn't. I was too shocked to move.

"I said turn it off!" Ray repeated. Keeping one hand over his eyes to block the light, he reached toward me with the other and shoved me, hard. I fell and landed sprawled on my back on the floor of the cave. Before Ray could do anything else to me, I turned off the flashlight and lay there for a moment, stunned and furious and humiliated.

As I slowly picked myself up, I could see Ray's skinny frame silhouetted against the cave's mouth. Now, I figured, he was blinded by the sudden plunge into darkness.

"So you want to go crying to the cops, huh?" Ray kept talking into the blackness.

Warily, I watched his arm move. He was reaching slowly into his shirt and laughing mockingly, saying, "Poor little babies are getting scared, is that it? Well, listen up."

But I didn't want to listen up. And I didn't want to find out what Ray was reaching for. I felt a rush of power and energy flood through me, fueled by anger at Ray and the need to stop his taunting voice, stop his reaching hand.

Moving quietly, I took two steps that brought me within reach of Ray, and snapped on the light, shining it full in his face. In the instant that he squinted his eyes shut and raised his hands to cover them, I swung the heavy flashlight and crashed it into his head as hard as I could.

Ray's knees buckled, and I felt him going down as the flashlight fell from my hands and went out. He lay in a crumpled heap in the doorway to the cave.

"Come on, Donny! Quick!" I called. "Before he gets up!"

Ray moaned, let out a curse, and began trying to struggle to his feet.

I stepped over him and started running down the cliffs toward the beach, waiting to hear Donny coming along behind me. When I didn't, I stopped. I could hear sounds of struggle from the cave. Then a figure appeared and began moving toward me. Donny!

Relieved, I began running again, wanting only to get to my bike, pedal to the police station, call home, and—

The night was shattered by a piercing blast. At first my mind couldn't make sense of what I was hearing. Then another blast followed the first, and I knew that what I'd heard was a gun. I knew it, but I couldn't quite believe it—*a gun*!

No! I thought. *Wait! No!*

Ray was shooting at us!

This couldn't be happening.

This was crazy.

"Donny!" I yelled. My voice carried across the cliffs, sounding high and panicky. "Donny! Are you all right?"

"Yeah." Donny pulled up behind me, panting. "Keep running! Go!"

I raced along, tripping, falling, tumbling, too panicked to notice or care, thinking only of the gun pointed in my direction, waiting for the crack of the trigger firing, the whistle of the bullet, the feel of it exploding into me, ending everything.

There was a *thunk* in the clay ahead of me, then another blast, and a bullet ricocheted off a nearby rock. I wanted to lie down and cover my head, but I knew I had to keep moving.

I could hear Donny still running right behind me. For all I knew, Ray was right behind *him,* closing in, waiting to get a clearer shot. My breath was coming in huge, rasping gulps and my legs felt wobbly from fear and fatigue, but I made myself run faster.

Finally, the steep slope of the cliffs gave way to flat, sandy beach. I ran down closer to the waterline, where I'd get a better foothold in the packed, wet sand, and kept running. I looked back just once and saw, to my relief, that Donny was still right behind me and there was no sign of Ray.

Did that mean we were safe? I didn't know. I had no idea of how far a gun could shoot, and no idea where Ray was.

Facing ahead once more, I thought I caught a glimpse of a light. Then again—yes, it was definitely a light—no, two lights. People were walking toward us, one with a flashlight and another holding a lantern. I heard voices. Probably fishermen. *Oh, thank you thank you thank you,* I thought. *Thank you.* But then along with relief came the thought: would Ray just shoot us all?

I could feel tears running down my face as I ran toward the light, and suddenly the beam was shining in my face and I stopped, gasping, blinded as Ray had been, and a familiar voice came out of the darkness.

"Ben?"

"*Mom?*"

"Ben! Thank goodness! Are you all right?"

I ran straight into Mom's outstretched arms and was about to let loose the sobs of fear that swelled in my chest. But Ray—and his gun—were still out there somewhere. Where was he? I grabbed the flashlight from Mom's hands and wheeled around to point it into the darkness.

Donny stood nearby, his breathing loud and ragged over the sound of the waves. I couldn't see anyone else, just the dark mounds of the dunes and the smooth sweep of sand stretching away into the areas beyond my torch's beam. Barry was with Mom, holding the lantern. The four of us stood for a moment, peering about uneasily.

"Shut off the lantern," I said to Barry as I turned off the flashlight. Ray might be close, and we didn't have to make targets of ourselves.

"Ben, what's going on?" Mom's voice held an edge of terror. "I thought I heard *gunshots*."

"I'll tell you later, Mom," I said. "But right now, we've got to *go*. Come on, *hurry*."

I wasn't used to giving orders and having people follow them, but there must have been something in my voice that made Mom and Barry understand that their questions had to wait. We raced the rest of the way up the beach, each of us stopping from time to time to look back. Mom and Barry didn't know what they were looking for, but Donny and I did, and that made our steps even quicker.

In the parking lot, we climbed into Barry's car, and he and Mom turned to me. "For heaven's sake, Ben. What's going on?"

I took a deep breath and replied, "Can we go right to the police station? I'll tell you everything there."

Twenty-one

AT THE STATION, Jeff's Uncle Cully was the desk
sergeant on duty. As soon as he heard we'd been shot at,
he called Chief Widdiss, who arrived within minutes. The
chief made some calls, including one to Donny's mother,
who showed up shortly afterward looking shaken and angry. He called the Mannings, too, and Jeff came with his
parents. I could tell from Jeff's face that he was really
scared.

A search was begun for Ray Nugent, whom, it turned
out, the police had been watching for a long time. Ray
had a drug-dealing record that went back to when he was
fifteen. He'd already been convicted twice, done jail time,
and been paroled. His new tactic had been to use young

kids like Jeff and me to actually make the exchange so he could deny any involvement.

We didn't find out all that right away, though. First the chief said, "Tell me about what happened tonight," and Donny and I began talking. It was a long time before we stopped.

Finally, the chief said we were finished for the night, but that there were going to be a lot more questions in the next couple of days. It was the district attorney's job to decide what charges would be brought against whom. That got me pretty nervous. But then the chief took Mom and me aside and said he thought Jeff and I might not get charged at all, because we hadn't known what was in the envelopes, because we were minors, and because I had come to him to tell what I knew.

I got the impression the chief considered Ray the really bad guy. Donny was kind of in the middle, and Jeff and I were just little fish, which was fine with me. Stupid little fish for sure. But at least we weren't treated like criminals.

The chief asked Donny a lot of questions about Ray and Cameron Maddox. Apparently, the coroner had said that the wound on Maddox's head had come from a blow at close range, probably from the butt of a gun. Ray was wanted for suspicion of murder, as well as for drug dealing.

I shuddered every time it hit me that I'd gotten myself

involved in something so big and so bad. It had been so *easy,* too, to take the first little step, and then the next and the next.

News came from the searchers that it looked as though Ray had stolen a boat and headed for the mainland. Chief Widdiss jumped to his feet. He told us we could go home, and started bellowing orders to get the state police and the Coast Guard on the phone right away.

"We're going to find this guy," he declared grimly as we left the station.

Donny and Jeff went home with their parents, and Mom, Barry, and I drove to our house in silence. Barry pulled into the driveway and said, "I'm going to leave and give you two a chance to talk this over."

Mom and I got out, and we both thanked Barry. "I'll call you in the morning, Kate," he said. "And, Ben, I'm glad you're safe."

Mom and I went inside and sat down at the kitchen table, the place where we'd always had our "big talks." Even though it was after midnight, I knew we weren't going to bed just yet. I was way too wired, anyway, and I could tell Mom had a lot more she wanted to say to me.

She poured me a glass of juice and boiled water for tea for herself. She began by saying, "Ben, I hardly know where to start. I find it hard to believe that all this has been going on, and I didn't know a thing about it." She shook her head, fighting back tears. Finally she whispered, "Honey, why didn't you tell me?"

I already felt so awful about everything that had happened, and now I felt worse, seeing Mom cry. I sighed, and opened my mouth to try to explain. But before I could say anything, she went on. "Actually, I think I understand most of it. I can see how you wanted to protect Donny, and how one thing led to another. But what upsets me is that I suspect in some ways you were trying to protect *me,* along with Donny."

Her eyes filled up and she wrapped her arms across her chest. "It's hard for me without your father, Ben, but you have to believe that I'm not going to fall apart at the first sign of trouble. You can count on me. You don't have to take on everything by yourself. Okay? Do you understand?"

"Yes, Mom," I said. And I did. We were still learning how to get along without Pop, and we didn't always get it right.

"Not talking to me about your troubles is bad enough, Ben, but you lied to me. That's the worst of it. Lying can change everything between people. Do you see that?"

I nodded miserably, because I really did understand it—now. First Ray sucked Donny in; then Donny sucked Jeff and me in. Donny had lied to us more than once. I wasn't mad at him so much as at myself for believing his lies.

Mom's face looked tired under the kitchen l̲. "The most important thing is that you're alive. But, B̲e̲. you've got some real hard thinking to do about why̲ you let yourself get into this situation. I feel as though I'̲ somehow, failed to teach you right from wrong. And when I think of how close you came—how much worse it could be—I—" Her face crumpled, and she turned away to pour hot water into her cup.

"I know," I said, swallowing the big lump that had risen in my throat. "Mom? Don't cry, okay? None of this was your fault. It's just that—" How could I explain this? I struggled for words that would make clear all the things I'd figured out. Finally I said, "You know how there's a little voice inside you that tells you when you're messing up? I heard it. I mean, it was *there,* but I didn't listen to it. I knew I should speak up, say no, ask questions, all that— but I didn't. Because . . . "

I listed all the stupid reasons. "Because I thought Donny was cool and I wanted him to like me. Because I didn't want Jeff to think I was a weenie. Because I wanted to impress other kids from school by hanging around with Donny. Because I want a boat and a motor and stuff we can't afford. Because I let Donny convince me the rules are different for islanders and other people." My voice trailed off, and I looked at Mom.

There was an odd expression on her face, a combination of anger, disappointment, love, and, I thought, even understanding. "Ben," she said softly, "it's late. We'll talk more about this tomorrow." Then she exclaimed suddenly, "Oh, my goodness! I forgot that you're working in the morning. After tonight, are you sure you should go?"

"Yeah," I said. "I'm sure." I didn't explain—and was suddenly too tired to explain—how much I wanted to go to work.

It felt like the only part of my life I hadn't messed up.

Twenty-two

O N M Y W A Y to the dock the next morning, I worried about how Chick was going to react. Had he already heard about what happened? And, if so, what did he think of me? To my relief, he acted perfectly normal, and I decided that when the day was over, I'd tell him the whole story myself.

It felt great to be out in the boat with Chick, fishing. Our clients were a lawyer from Ohio and his two sons, who were fourteen and fifteen. Even though they were older than I was, they'd never been fishing before. The bonito were breaking all around us, and I showed them how to aim their casts and how to work the lures we were using, giving them just the right action to drive the fish crazy.

"You listen to Ben," Chick told them. "He'll have you catching fish in no time."

It was good to be doing something right for a change. When I was fishing, everything made sense. In a boat, I knew what to do and how to do it. On dry land, things got more complicated.

Sure enough, pretty soon both Luke and Greg had hooked up nice fish, and they shouted and whooped with excitement as they reeled. They sounded just the way Jeff and I did when the action got hot.

Greg's fish made a sudden run, and the reel screamed as the fish took out line. I could see Greg was about to tighten the drag.

"Let him run!" I said quickly. "He'll break off if you try to stop him."

I showed Greg how to keep a slight amount of tension on the fish, enough to slow it down, but not enough to let it break off. I explained that we were only using a light, six-pound-test, monofilament line. Light line didn't spook the fish, but it meant he had to be careful, especially since this fish looked like a beauty. It was probably bigger than six pounds.

When Greg had successfully gotten the fish to the boat, I reached over the side, gaffed it, and handed it to him. He held it up and posed, his face flushed red with triumph, while his father took a picture.

"Thanks, man; that was awesome!" Greg said, and turned to give me a high five. "How'd you learn to fish like that?"

I shrugged, embarrassed but also pleased. Luckily, Luke's fish chose that moment to make a run, and I didn't have to answer.

By lunchtime Luke, Greg, and I were having a blast. They didn't need any more coaching from me, and their dad told me to get a rod and fish, too. I looked at Chick, who smiled and nodded.

"Go ahead, Ben," he said. "These fish seem determined to commit suicide. You might as well help 'em. Why don't you use my fly rod?"

After we'd fished for a while, Greg said, "We've got plenty for dinner. What do we do now?"

"Keep fishing!" I said. "But we'll let 'em go from now on."

We caught and released about seven more bonito and a few albacore before it was time to head in. At the dock, Luke and Greg wanted to help me clean the fish, so I filleted one to show them how. They thought cleaning fish was fun, so I gladly "let them" finish the rest while I watched.

Donny had talked about sharing the wealth. He had his ideas about it, and I had mine. I didn't mind sharing the island with guys like Greg and Luke. I didn't care where they were from. They loved fishing, and so did I. *And cleaning fish is part of fishing,* I thought, grinning to myself.

Before they left, they signed up for another day's fishing with Chick the following week.

"You'll be here, too, Ben?" Greg asked.

I looked to Chick for an answer.

"Sure thing," Chick said. "Can't fish without my first mate."

I hoped he'd still feel the same way later, when I had told him what I had to say.

After thanking us about a million times and saying they'd see us next week, Greg and Luke and their dad left, and I turned to Chick. "Chick, I've got something to tell you, and after I tell you, if you don't want me to mate for you anymore, it's okay."

Chick looked up from the stern line he was securing to the dock. "I stopped at the Texaco for coffee this morning, Ben, and I think I already know what you're going to tell me. What I'd like to know is, why do you think I wouldn't want you to mate for me anymore?"

I was stunned. "You *know*?"

Chick laughed. "Come on, Ben. You know how fast news travels on this island. I heard the whole story. There were about ten of us there, including two guys from the police force."

"So—" I stopped to get my thoughts together. "Aren't you mad? Or disappointed? What do you *think*?"

"I'd say the more important question is, what do *you* think?"

I looked down at the deck. I had so many thoughts, I hardly knew where to start. I summed it up by saying, "I think I really screwed up."

"Okay," Chick said, "so you screwed up. Lots of people make mistakes, and they can't admit it. Do you think I've never done anything really dumb? Do you think Jack Daggett never screwed up?"

"No, but—"

"Just listen for a second, Ben. You made some choices that weren't so smart. You got yourself into something way over your head. But once you realized it, what did you do?"

"I nearly got Donny and me killed, for one thing," I said.

"You're determined to be hard on yourself, aren't you? I guess there's nothing wrong with that. But, Ben, the way I heard it, once you knew about the drugs, you tried to do the right thing. You intended to go to the police, but first you wanted to warn Donny and give him a chance to come clean, too. You didn't know that Ray character was going to show up and start shooting. You put yourself at risk for Donny, because you thought of him as your friend. You can say it was stupid if you want, but I think what you did took courage. Can't you see that?"

I. couldn't, not right then. But Chick's words spread through me like a warm current.

"From what I understand, you're going to have to spend a lot of time over summer vacation straightening this thing out. When they catch Ray Nugent, you and Jeff and Donny are all going to have to testify at the trial, and there's going to be all kinds of legal shenanigans.

"But I want you here working for me every day you can, you hear?"

Tears flooded my eyes, and there was no way I could get words past the hard lump in my throat. I nodded.

"Here," said Chick, handing me my pay. "Give me a call tonight after you talk to Chief Widdiss. If he doesn't need you tomorrow, I do."

I put the money in my pocket and turned away, wishing I knew how to tell Chick how grateful I was but hoping he knew, anyway.

It felt good to ride home with thirty dollars in my pocket, money that I had earned fishing, just the way Pop had.

Twenty-three

BEFORE I KNEW IT, it was the end of July and the summer was half over. Between working for Chick and meeting with Chief Widdiss and the district attorney, I was busy every second. But one Sunday morning I found myself with nothing I had to do. Chick's motor was acting up and he was going to spend the day working on it, and it seemed the lawyers and police had gotten all the information they needed from me for a while.

Mom and Barry wanted to go to the beach, so I called Jeff to see if he could come along with us.

"Good," I said, after his mom had given him permission. "Bring your plane, and we'll give 'er another shot."

We spread our towels on the sand and sat for a while, watching the people and the water and enjoying the feel of the sun and the cool, salty air. The ocean was calm, and the waves were coming in as long smooth rollers.

"Look at those little boys on their rafts," Mom said. "They remind me of you two when you were that age. You'd stay in for hours, until you were blue. 'Don't you want to come in and warm up?' I'd ask. 'W-we're n-not c-cold,' you'd say, shivering so hard you could barely talk."

I looked at Jeff and we both smiled. I knew what he was thinking. *Moms.*

Barry was laughing. "What happens to us when we get old? I used to be the same way. Now I'm perfectly content to sit here and watch those kids do the swimming."

"Aw, come on in with us, Barry," I teased.

"Maybe in a while when I'm good and hot," he said. "I thought you guys were going to fly that plane."

"We are," I said lazily. For the moment, it felt good to just lie there, doing nothing. I looked up at the clay cliffs, their colors brilliant in the sunshine. Gulls and large dragonflies cruised the rim, effortlessly riding the warm air that rose from the cliff's shimmering surface. It was so beautiful and peaceful, I could hardly believe this was the same place where, not long ago, Ray had been shooting at me.

I gazed out at Devil's Bridge. The waves were breaking gently on the rocks while the gulls stood guard and a few eider ducks poked about in the shallows. In my mind,

Devil's Bridge had always been the spot where Pop caught his big record-holding striped bass. Now it was also the place where Jeff and I had found a kid's body.

The sea, which today appeared so mild and harmless, was the same sea that had swallowed Pop and Cameron Maddox. The fury of Hurricane Lois had caused Pop's death. Drugs and alcohol—and Ray Nugent—had led Maddox to his watery end on the rocks of Devil's Bridge.

They'd found the stolen boat ditched over on the mainland, and not long after that they'd found Ray. A grand jury was going to decide if there was enough evidence to try Ray for murder. The district attorney said not to worry, there was plenty. There would be another trial, as well, for drug trafficking. Jeff and I were going to be witnesses. In exchange for our testimony and our cooperation, no charges would be brought against us.

I felt really lucky. Of course, I was still dealing with the charges I'd brought against myself, and I guessed it would be a while before the shame went away. Still, every day I worked for Chick, I felt a little better.

Donny was in more serious trouble. His parents had hired a lawyer, and we still didn't know what was going to happen, except that he'd probably have to do some time in jail. The Porsche was valuable property, and he'd destroyed it. Robbing the boat was a felony, which was a big-deal crime. Then there was the whole drug thing with

Ray, and no one was sure yet where the blame for that would fall. And, of course, Donny'd lost Jen, too.

Jeff interrupted my daydreaming. "You want to try this thing out?"

"Sure," I said, getting up from my towel. "The wind is perfect, don't you think? Off the ocean, but not too strong."

"Yeah," said Jeff. "Looks good."

"Better go over there," said Mom, pointing down the beach. "Away from all these people."

"Okay."

Carefully we got everything ready, cranked up the engine, and let 'er go. I could tell Jeff was nervous at first, but the plane flew like a bird. Soon we had it doing rolls and loops out over the water, and a crowd gathered to watch. Everybody was whooping and hollering and pointing. Jeff and I took turns at the controls, and I guess we began showing off a little, with all those people watching.

Jeff was putting the plane through a particularly tricky maneuver when it began to sputter. One minute it was climbing upward through the clear blue sky, the next it veered wildly off course and began plummeting toward the sea. A cry went up from the crowd, ending in a moan of relief as the plane pulled out of the sharp dive, evened out, and landed roughly in the shallow water near shore.

"Oh, man!" cried Jeff. "What happened?"

"I don't know," I said, wading out into the waves with him to examine the plane. The right wing was broken, and the tail was bent pretty far to the left.

"At least it's not totally wrecked," he said.

"You can fix it, can't you?" I asked.

Jeff nodded, still inspecting the damage intently. "Yeah. It won't be easy. I'll have to put an extra strut here," he said, pointing to the wing. "But with a little glue and a new paper job, she could be as good as new."

"Maybe even better than before," I said. "Stronger."

"Yeah."

We were quiet for a minute, looking at the plane. Then we picked up the pieces and carried them back to our towels.

"Okay," I said, turning to Barry with a grin. "Ready for a swim?"

He surprised me by jumping up and making a mad dash for the ocean. Laughing, we watched him run through the first few waves and dive under a big one. Then Jeff and Mom and I all raced in after him.

The cold, salty water felt great. I caught the first breaker and bodysurfed it all the way in to shore. I headed back out to catch another wave. This time I let its foamy force tumble me over and over. Then I straightened out and shot up from the water into the warm summer air.